LITTLE WORDS OF WISDOM

Andrew Dart has a Master's Degree in Research Psychology from Anglia Ruskin University in Cambridge. His previous titles include *Building your Skeptical Toolkit*, a beginner's guide to science, skepticism, and critical thinking skills. He is part of the team that runs Cambridge Skeptics, a not-for-profit community organization promoting science, positive skepticism, and critical thinking skills via public engagement. Andrew lives in a small village near Ely with his partner Ellen and their cats, Millie and Lulu. This is his first novel.

Find out more about the author at www.andrewdart.co.uk. Find out more about Cambridge Skeptics at www.cambridgeskeptics.org.uk.

Also by Andrew Dart

NON FICTION:

Building your Skeptical Toolkit

CHILDREN'S BOOKS:

Why is the Sky Blue?

Little Words of Wisdom

ANDREW DART

Copyright © 2021 Andrew Dart

No reproduction without permission.

All rights reserved.

Andrew Dart asserts the moral right to be identified as the author of this work

This book is a work of fiction. Names, characters, places, and incidents are either a product of the author's imagination or are used fictitiously. Any resemblance to actual persons, living or dead, events, or locales is entirely coincidental.

www.andrewdart.co.uk

First Printed: November 2021

ISBN: 9798752429361

Created with
Amazon Kindle Direct Publishing

For The Fountain Writers
So then, who's next?

ACKNOWLEDGMENTS

I want to say a massive thank you to all the people who have had a hand in bringing this novel to life. Wesley, for all the time we have spent walking and talking about writing, and for helping to generate the spark that became this story.

All the wonderful people who make up The Fountain Writers, a group of smart, funny, and incredibly talented people who for some reason let me hang around with them.

Ellen, for putting up with me and the roller-coaster of moods that writing brings out in me. That and everything else of course.

To my family for always being so supportive and believing I would actually finish a story even when I didn't.

Special thanks to Claire, Jacqui, and Julia, for acting as my amazing editorial team. Any remaining unnecessary "just"s and "then"s are entirely down to me.

And lastly you, the reader, for taking a chance on a self-published novel. I can't tell you how much I appreciate it, and I hope you enjoy the story.

1

"A visitor will come with unexpected news, and things will never be the same again."
The Wisdom of Zhu Zhuang, No. 532

It's funny how you can forget the sound of your own doorbell.

It was dark outside and I was well into my wind down routine for the day. A two-thirds full cup of hot chocolate was vying for space amongst the empty mugs on the end table beside me and I was a few short pages away from closing my book for the evening and heading up to bed. My cat was already a step ahead of me, snoring softly to herself atop a pile of bills and unopened letters on the sofa beside me and completely oblivious to the sudden chimes of the doorbell. Likewise my dog was sprawled out in a decidedly undignified manner in front of the empty fire place, though he'd at least deigned to raise an ear at the sound. The doorbell sounded again, something distinctly insistent about the soft sound coming as it did at this late hour of night. I looked at my two animals in turn again, neither of whom showed any sign of pending movement, and with a sigh I slipped the old rail ticket I was using as a bookmark between the pages of my novel and placed it down next to my cat.

"Ok, well I guess I'll get that then shall I?" I said to the animals as a hauled myself up off the sofa.

Bob, my shaggy old golden retriever, raised his head and looked up at me.

"No, no, you stay here, I've got this," I said, making a patting action with my hand.

Bob immediately lay his big head back down again, apparently deciding to actually obey one of my instructions first time for once in his life, and I headed out of the living room and into the unlit hallway beyond. My eyes were drawn immediately to the flashing red light on my answer machine and I pressed the 'erase message' button almost without thinking about it. Some people just didn't get the message; no pun intended. Moving on I was almost at the door when the bell sounded once more.

"Yes, yes," I called out, "I'm coming, keep your hair on."

I grabbed up my keys from the ceramic bowl on the hall table and set about unlocking the door. I could make out the silhouette of a large figure bathed in the harsh glare of my security light through the doors frosted glass panes, but no more detail than that. Keeping the chain in place and the key in the lock I cracked the door open a couple of inches and peered out into the night.

"Yes, how can I help you?" I asked.

A quick look of surprise mixed with confusion crossed the face of the large man on the porch, who I most definitely did not know, before it was quickly buried beneath a mask of confident professionalism. He was smartly dressed, his functional looking suit and tie ensemble framed by a long black rain coat that, despite there only being a slight mist of rain in the air, was already proving itself to be a sensible addition to his outfit. He looked to be about ten years older than me, with pronounced areas of grey at the temples of his short dark hair and a face that appeared worn by both hard work and hard times. He was a long day shy of clean shaven, had impressively bushy eyebrows and his wide mouth was pressed into a tight, almost lipless line. He stared at me through the crack in the door for a moment as if deciding what to do next, and then brought up his right hand and held something out in front of him for me to see.

"I'm DI Fuller, Metropolitan Police Service, could I have a moment of your time please sir?"

My eyes flickered from the man's face to what I could now see was a warrant card held out before him, something I only recognised from the inordinate amount of crime drama I watched on TV these days, and I immediately started to feel my heart beat faster in my chest. I had no direct experience of this sort of thing, but whenever DIs Frost, Lewis, or Pascoe turned up at someone's door late at night it was never good news. My first thought was that there had been some sort of terrible accident, but I couldn't think of anyone I was close enough to for the police to inform me both personally and late at night of their passing. My second instinct was that I had unknowingly committed a crime, but given that I worked from home and really only left the house to walk Bob and go to the shops this seemed even more unlikely. I swallowed down the growing lump in my throat and decided that the quickest way to an answer was to just ask.

"Um, sure, yes, how can I help?" I said in a voice that sounded slightly off pitch to me.

Fuller slipped his warrant card back into his pocket, looked me in the eye for a moment and then shot a conspicuous look at the door. I felt my face redden.

"Sorry, of course," I said, before closing the door, removing the chain lock, and opening it again more fully.

Fuller nodded appreciatively, though the look of

slight confusion had returned to his face. He glanced past me down the dark hallway as if expecting to see someone else lurking in the shadows, before returning his attention to me. He pulled a small black notebook from the inside pocket of his suit jacket, flipped through a few pages before looking back up at me.

"I'm sorry to bother you so late like this sir; I was hoping to speak to a Mr..." he checked his notes again, "Shoo Shang, if he is available?"

I felt my face race through a number of different reactions. A quick wince at the terrible mispronunciation, a flash of confusion as to why the police would have that name, and finally a small smile at the fact that, despite the late hour, this was highly unlikely to be about anything serious.

"It's Zhu Zhuang," I said correcting the pronunciation, "and that's me."

Fuller's eyebrows climbed momentarily up onto his forehead before he brought his surprise back under control. He looked at me sceptically.

"You're Zhu Zhuang?"

I nodded.

"That's right, how can I help you?"

Fuller paused for a moment, took a small step back and ran his gaze quickly up and down my body. I could well imagine his confusion at what he saw. I am, I'm somewhat hesitant to admit, decidedly white, middle-aged, and middle class in appearance. I was dressed in a thick, dark blue fleece jumper, over a slightly lighter blue polo shirt, and had on a pair of worn denim jeans. My light brown hair was in need of a cut, and much like Fuller I was sporting a five o'clock shadow, though in fact mine was the result of more than a single day of not shaving. Had I been wearing wellington boots rather than a pair of checked slippers, the most grandfatherly of slippers, I would have looked right at home on the cover of Farmers Weekly, assuming they put people on the cover, which I didn't know as I had never read a copy. What I most certainly did not look like was any manner of Oriental. Fuller seemed to consider that I might be messing with him and so asked again.

"Your name is Zhu Zhuang?"

I nodded.

"Yes," I replied.

Then I shook my head.

"Well no, Zhu Zhuang is my pen name, my real name's Steven Lander," I held out my hand, immediately feeling foolish for doing so, "but please call me Steve."

Fuller glanced at the hand, left if long enough to make me feel even more uncomfortable, and then reached out and shook it.

"Nice to meet you Mr Lander," he said his voice still full of questions, "but for the record you are confirming that you also go by the alias Zhu Zhuang?"

I smiled at this.

"Goodness, alias makes it sound so nefarious, it's nothing like that. I simply use the name as a part of my side job, gives it the right sort of ambience you know? It's what people expect."

Fuller seemed to think about this for a moment before nodding his head in acceptance.

"Makes sense," he said, "certainly fits better than Steven Lander, no offence."

"None taken," I replied, with a quick reassuring raise of the hand.

A sudden gust of wind came in through the door, bringing with it a fine spray of the misty rain, and I was suddenly reminded that it was night time and that my hot chocolate was getting cold.

"Look, do you mind me asking what this is all about? It is rather late for you to be showing up like this unannounced."

"Of course, I'm sorry about that. I have a few questions I'd like to ask you about your side business if that would be ok with you Mr Lander?"

I let out a sigh, my interest in the whole matter waning by the moment.

"Can it not wait until the morning?" I asked.

Fuller took a deep breath.

"Of course, but I've driven all the way out here from London to speak to you Mr Lander; I would appreciate it greatly if you would take some time to answer some of my questions."

I sighed again and nodded. Fuller paused for a moment and then gestured slightly with his chin.

"Inside if possible," he said.

I waited long enough to show I was not best pleased with the whole situation, but not long enough to be rude, and invited him in. I am British after all, showing my disapproval whilst being polite is something that comes naturally. I closed the door behind him and led him through to the living room. Dumping a small pile of unread magazines off the sofa and onto the floor I gestured for him to take a seat. Bob's head came up at the sight of a stranger and he gave his tail a couple of quick wags. I sat back in my usual place and Bob clambered to his feet, walked over and sat back down, resting his big head heavily on my lap in what I knew was a protective gesture. For her part my black and white cat Tortoise, don't ask it's the name she came with, opened her eyes, gave a wide yawn showing a surprising number of teeth, before getting to her feet, walking over to Fuller and giving him a quick sniff. Apparently satisfied she rubbed her head against his leg, marking him as her property, then hopped down from the sofa and sauntered silently out of the room.

"So Detective Fuller," I said as I scratched Bob's head between his ears, "what do you want to ask me?"

Fuller suddenly seem to become uncomfortable and his bearing lost a little of the forthright certainty it had held moments before. He looked at his notebook again, flicking through a few pages as if seeking reassurance in the words written there.

"I," he said then paused again in a manner that immediately made me feel that whatever it was he wanted to talk to me about it was something deeply personal to him. "I must admit that now that I'm here I am not entirely sure where the best place to start is."

I shrugged as if it didn't really matter to me.

"How about you start by telling me why you came all this way to see me in the middle of the night?"

He looked up at me and after a second I saw resolve enter his eyes.

"I am here," he said, his voice every inch that of a professional police office again, "because I am pretty sure you saved my son's life."

2

"Wise words from the past will carry new meaning in the present."
The Wisdom of Zhu Zhuang, No. 752

Now I've done a lot of things in my life. Well, no, not really, but I have done enough. I'd graduated top of my class at university. I'd started my own successful one man architecture company, and I had won first place in the county baking competition a few years back. As such I felt pretty accomplished in my own way. However, one thing I was fairly certain I had never done was save anyone's life, and most definitely not that of anyone who could reasonably be considered the son of the large policeman currently sitting across from me on the sofa.

"I beg your pardon," I said leaning forward slightly, "but I have no idea what you're talking about."

Fuller looked away from me and cast his eyes around my dishevelled living room.

"Do you live here alone?" he asked, changing the subject.

I shifted slightly in my seat.

"Yes, well apart from the fur babies that is," I said, giving Bob's neck a quick pat.

Fuller looked back at me with a slight raise of his eyebrows. God, why had I just referred to my pets as fur babies in front of a police officer? Apparently I had turned into a six year old girl.

"No Mrs Lander?"

A familiar stab of pain struck me at this and I felt my insides involuntarily tighten. I swallowed.

"No, not anymore," I said a slight croak to my voice.

Fuller looked at me for a moment and I suddenly found I couldn't meet his eye. After a second he nodded to himself in recognition.

"I'm sorry for your loss Mr Lander," He said with what sounded like genuine condolence.

I shrugged.

"Not your fault," I replied in that stupid way people do.

I sniffed and rubbed quickly at my eyes. I could

feel the waters rising behind my emotional dam. I was tired and rapidly losing my patience with this whole thing.

"Look, fun as all this is, I am pretty sure you've got the wrong guy. I didn't save your son's life. I've never met you before, I seriously doubt if I've ever met him. You're from London right, and I haven't been there in years, and I am pretty sure the last time I went to the Natural History Museum I didn't save anyone's life. So I am sorry you came all the way out here in the middle of the night to see me, but I can't help you, I'm not the person you're looking for."

Fuller let me finish my little rant before reaching into the pocket of his rain coat that, I now realised, was dripping onto my sofa, and pulled out a small, labelled plastic bag that I immediately recognised as an evidence bag, thank you BBC crime drama. He held it in his hands for a second as if reluctant to hand it over before, with a deep breath, passing it to me.

"Take a look," He said.

I took the bag and turned it over in my hands. The bag was about the size of my iPad and was all but empty. It held only two small, narrow rectangles of what looked like paper. I recognised them immediately. I knew their exact dimensions, one centimetre by five, I knew that they were in fact made of a fairly expensive vellum rather than paper, and I knew the exact brand of calligraphy ink used to adorn their surface. I knew all of this because at some point in the past I had painstakingly crafted them myself in the small room at the rear of my house. I looked up at Fuller expectantly, unsure where all this was going.

"Those are yours, correct?" he asked.

I nodded.

"Yes, I mean they are a couple of years old now, I switched to using a different base parchment a little over a year back, but yes, I made these. Where did you get them?"

Rather than answer, Fuller gestured towards the bag.

"Take them out, read them," He said.

I turned the evidence bag over and found that it hadn't been sealed shut so it was a job of seconds to open it and pour the contents into my waiting hand. I put the bag to one side and held the two small piece of vellum, one on top of the other, before me. I was surprised to see how good a condition they were in given their age. While I made them out of some of the best materials available they weren't exactly made to last. In general I expected them to provide a few minutes of entertainment at most before they were discarded and forgotten, eventually finding their way into a landfill somewhere. I most certainly did not expect to find them bagged, preserved, and presented back to me many months later. I looked at the words written on the top one and recognised my own flamboyant penmanship, a little rough at the edges compared to what I could manage these days, but unmistakably mine. I glanced at Fuller, who nodded back in a clear 'please continue' gesture, and so I read the first one out loud.

"Big decisions are best left until the light of day. Put this one off until tomorrow. The Wisdom of Zhu Zhuang, number 325."

I swapped the pieces of vellum round so that the bottom one was now on the top. I looked at Fuller again, my confusion growing.

"Read the other one," he said in an almost cajoling manner, "please."

It was clearly important to him that I read them out loud, so I looked down again and, clearing my throat, read.

"All your wishes will come true; just wait for the morning light. The Wisdom of Zhu Zhuang, number 319."

I looked at Fuller again who was watching me with a clearly expectant expression.

"I don't understand," I said. "These are two of the fortunes I wrote for the cookies I make. Why do you have them, and what does this have to do with me apparently saving the life of your son?"

Fuller's shoulders slumped visibly. He had clearly been expecting something different from me and I had disappointed him.

"You're saying you don't know?" he said, the tiniest traces of anger at the edges of his words.

I sat up a little straighter, unconsciously moving myself a little further away from him, and shook my head.

"I'm sorry, I don't think I can help you. Look I really have no idea what this is all about. Yes, I made these; I am not denying that. But they are just fortune cookie fortunes. I've made hundreds of these things. They are simply meaningless platitudes, nothing more. Can you please tell me what this is all about?"

Fuller sighed then reached out and picked up the evidence bag. He held out his hand to me and, somewhat reluctantly I will admit, I handed the two fortunes back to him. He took them a little forcefully, popped them back in the bag, folded it neatly and stuffed in back deep into the pocket of his rain coat.

"I'm sorry, but if you're not going to be straight with me about what you know then this is all a waste of time," he growled as he started to rise.

Now I could feel my own temper rising and, pushing Bob's head to one side and receiving a grumbled whine in the process, I was on my feet before him.

"Now wait a minute," I said my voice a little louder than I'd intended. "You've come all the way out here to bother me and now you're going to leave without telling me anything? And why, because I don't know what my fortune cookies have to do with your son? Well maybe if you gave me a few more details I might be able to fill in the blanks. It's either that or yes, you have wasted both of our times."

Fuller looked at me and I swallowed. I immediately remembered that he was a policeman and that I probably shouldn't be speaking to him like that. But after a moment he seemed to relax a little and lowered himself back onto the sofa.

"You're right," he said. "I owe you more of an explanation than I have given so far."

I let out a held breath.

"Well ok," I said in what I hoped was a reasonable tone, "that's, that's very good."

I sat back down awkwardly. Bob looked at me for a second, made another grumbling sound, and lay his head down on the floor. Guess I was on my own now then. Served me right I guess. I sat there expectantly, looking over at Fuller. For his part he suddenly seemed very interested in his lap and again I was struck by the thought that this whole thing was extremely important to him. I also found myself wondering for the first time if he was actually here on anything related to official police business.

"A little over two years ago," he said suddenly making me jump a little, "my son was involved in a motorcycle accident."

He sniffed and closed his eyes.

"It was his own fault really. It was raining, visibility was bad, and he was going too fast. He always went too fast," he paused and took a breath. "Anyway, a car pulled out of a side street, I'm sure you can fill in the rest."

I felt my muscles tighten a little at this. I could imagine it all too easily and even the thought of it felt awful. Having it happen to someone you cared about must have been devastating. The irritation I had been feeling towards Fuller disappeared in an instant.

"The damage to his heart was extensive. The doctors did everything they could of course. He was in surgery for what felt like an eternity, certainly much longer than I would have expected. They managed to repair most of the damage, goddamn miracle workers if you ask me, but at the end of it all his heart still wasn't beating."

He sniffed again and looked up at the ceiling for a moment. After a second he turned and looked at me for the first time since he had started the story and his eyes were like cold stone. As someone who had first-hand experience with the sudden, unexpected loss of a loved one I could well understand the sort of emotions he was no doubt struggling to contain. But whereas I dealt with it with an overly abundant amount of sarcasm and by throwing myself into strange hobbies to an almost obsessive level, Fuller clearly took a different approach. He dealt with the emotions by beating them down, cuffing them and throwing them into a cell made of anger and will and solid, unshakeable professionalism. As someone who had journeyed to the edge myself I could recognise a fellow traveller, but I doubted that anyone who had not been through what we had would have seen anything other than a strong, angry man without an inch of give in him. If I hadn't just heard his story I would have been scared of Fuller right at that moment. He let out a clearly forced cough and continued.

"It was only the machines keeping him alive at that point, and the doctors were saying that without an organ donor it was very unlikely he would live more than a few days. I don't know if you know this, but they don't like to keep people on those things for too long, too high a risk of infection you see. Plus of course Chris, did I tell you his name? Well Chris was an organ donor himself. And while they never said anything directly, never put any pressure on, there was this unspoken suggestion that he could be saving someone else's life."

He rubbed his hands together.

"And of course it is what he would have wanted. He wouldn't have wanted to be attached to all those machines when he could have been helping someone. Hell when I was his age all I cared about was girls and football, but not him, not Chris. No he wanted to go work with poor people out in Africa or some such place, always going on about some cause or another. Don't know where he got it from, certainly wasn't me."

He took a deep breath as if preparing for what he

would say next.

"And so we decided to pull the plug."

He looked me dead in the eye for a moment as if daring me to question his decision. I said nothing.

"Well," he continued, pointedly looking away, "at least that is what we planned on doing."

I could feel myself almost holding my breath at this point, more invested in the story than I had any real right to be. I was thinking about this strong man standing over the bed of his dying son and trying to make the decision that he thought his son would have wanted. I was thinking of him, but I was picturing Laci. At least Fuller had had a choice.

"Anyway, we needed to get out of there for a bit, take a walk, get some air you know. Plus back then I was a heavy smoker and I was gonna kill someone if I didn't get a fix soon. So we left the hospital and just sort of wandered around the streets. After a bit it started to rain, really piss it down, real typical British summer weather, you know the sort."

I nodded as it seemed the right thing to do.

"We found ourselves seeking shelter in this little Chinese restaurant in Whitechapel called the Golden Phoenix. You know it?"

I could tell from the look in his eyes and the way he made the words sound more like a statement than a question that he knew I did. I had never actually been there myself, but it was one of only a very few restaurants around the country that I had sold my fortune cookies to, before the demand became too much for me to keep up with and I'd recently switched to making them for private events only.

"I know it," I said quietly.

Fuller raised his eyebrows slightly as though I had made some big admission and continued.

"They weren't going to let us simply stand around in the foyer dripping on everything, so we got a table even though neither of us felt like eating. We ordered a few things, I have no idea what, I think I got a beer, maybe more than one, and Helen, that's my wife, sat there nursing a glass of wine and crying on and off. Anyway the rain stopped and we both knew it was time to go back, time to go kill our son."

I took a breath at the way he so casually said this, but Fuller didn't seem to notice, or maybe he did and didn't care.

"So they brought the bill over and there they were. Two of your fortune cookies."

He actually smiled a little at this.

"I must say Mr Landers, you do good work, the way you present them like that, makes them, oh I don't know, little works of art, or is that me being silly?"

I didn't answer, but I felt a small glow of pride at his description.

"Like I said, neither of us was hungry, but there was simply something about those two little cookies, they just seemed too good to waste. I mean a plate of rice and Hong Kong chicken balls, you can get them on any street in London, but these fortune cookies, they were something different, something special. We both felt we had to at least read what they had inside."

I found my eyes drawn to the pocket into which he had placed the evidence bag. I could tell what was coming next.

"Anyway Helen about broke down right there and then when she read hers, and I am not too big to admit that I felt like doing the same thing myself. I got angry too, felt like storming into the kitchen and demanding to know what they were playing at. Well, as you can imagine, it got real awkward in there real fast and so I dumped down a handful of notes and we got out of there."

He sniffed again and this time rubbed at his nose with the back of his hand.

"We walked back to the hospital in silence, pretty much like we were both walking on our own. So we got to Chris's room and the doctor came to see and ask if we had made a decision. Now as I said we both knew what Chris would have wanted and the truth is we had made a decision, we both knew what we were going to say before we had gone for that walk. Instead we looked at each other and knew we had both changed our minds. So I told the doctor no, that we needed more time, and Helen said 'wait until tomorrow'. And that was that. The doctor went off to see his other patients and we settled down to try and get some sleep for what we both felt was the last night of our son's life."

He swallowed and I saw a flash of wetness at the corner of those stone eyes.

"A little after 3am Chris's heart started beating on its own."

I let out a small gasp and despite only having just met this man and never having met his son a sudden wave of emotion threatened to overwhelm me and I had to turn my head away as I fought to rein it back in.

"Of course the doctors had lots of technical words to describe it, and kept going on about probabilities and all that, but I'm telling you that's as close to a real miracle as I've ever seen."

He smiled, his eyes focusing on some distant memory.

"Took him a long time to recover, and a couple more operations, but he made it, he made it. Got married a few months back, some girl he met in rehab, lovely little thing, only one leg."

He lifted his head and suddenly his eyes were locked on mine again.

"If it weren't for your fortune cookies my son would be dead right now, and I would have killed him. You saved his life."

He took a deep breath.

"And I want to know how you did it."

3

"The truth can be hard to swallow, but that doesn't make it any less true."
The Wisdom of Zhu Zhuang, No. 125

I sat there in silence for what seemed to me like an inordinately long time just staring at Fuller. How on earth I was meant to respond to something like that? His story had touched me deeply, in no small part because I related to it so strongly. I knew the kind of pain he had been through, and while my own story had ended very differently I could easily imagine the sheer overpowering sense of joy and relief he would have experienced at his son's recovery. All that made sense to me. What I most definitely did not get however was this implication that I had not simply influenced his decision in an indirect manner, but that I had somehow known it was all going to happen and had acted intentionally to produce a favourable outcome. And I had apparently done so via custom made fortune cookies.

"Look," I said softly, worried I might again ignite Fuller's anger, "I am really, really happy that everything worked out well for you and your son, I really am. And the fact that, in some small way, something I did helped you to make what turned out to be the right decision, well, I can't really describe how that makes me feel, it's amazing. And the fact that you would track me down and come out to tell me your story in person, even if you don't have the best timing, is deeply touching, and I thank you for doing so. Honestly, it means a lot that you have told me this. But this idea that I did it on purpose, I'm sorry, but that's just not the case."

Fuller looked at me in silence for a moment before letting out a breath he had apparently been holding. He nodded his head slightly and I felt tension that I hadn't realised was there start to ease from my shoulders. Then his eyes locked on mine again.

"I don't believe you," He said.

"What?" I said, incredulity clear in my voice. "What do you mean you don't believe me?"

Fuller shrugged.

"Just that, I don't believe you. Sure, I believe the things you said about being happy for me, that all rings true. But the rest, I'm sorry Mr Lander, but I think you're lying to me."

I practically snorted at this.

"So what, what do you think happened? Do you think that I somehow predicted the future or something? And then, rather than trying to find a way to contact you directly or let you know through some other less convoluted way, I instead wrote down what I wanted to tell you in as vague a way as possible, baked my prediction into a fortune cookie and sent them off to a restaurant that I've never been to on the off chance that you would go there and be given that exact fortune right at the moment you needed it most? Does that even sound remotely plausible to you?"

Fuller shrugged again.

"I don't know, you tell me. Is that how you did it?"

I threw up my hands. I couldn't believe this was happening again, and that it was coming from a policeman of all people. This is why I had stopped making fortune cookies for people I knew, choosing instead to operate through the anonymity of the internet under an alias. I got fed up with people reading more into my fortunes than was actually there.

"I didn't do anything," I said the volume of my voice increasing slightly once more. "It's a coincidence, that's it. It's a wonderful coincidence, maybe the best coincidence ever. I don't know, I don't keep track of these things, but that is all it is, a coincidence."

I pointed at the pocket into which Fuller had placed the bag containing the two fortunes.

"Get them out again, look at them."

Fuller didn't move for a moment and then reached, with exaggerated reluctance, into his pocket and drew out the bag. He flipped it over and looked at the two fortunes through the clear plastic.

"See those numbers?" I said, gesturing at the bag again. "What were they? 319 and 325, something like that?"

Fuller nodded; his eyes now on me rather than the contents of the bag.

"Well that means I wrote them pretty close together, undoubtedly on the same day. Heck I could check if you really want me to, I keep a record of the all fortunes I come up with. The point is that when I have an idea for a fortune I tend to write multiple different fortunes along the same theme. Things will be better tomorrow. Heck I could probably real off twenty different ways of saying that right now, without even having to think about it that much. I'd be genuinely surprised if I wrote less than thirty different versions of that sentiment for my cookies. I then stick all the finished fortunes into a bowl and draw them out at random and add them to the new batch of cookies I'm making. After that I box up the finished cookies and send them off to whoever has ordered them, that's it. I have no control over what happens to them after that, no idea who is going to get which fortune. At best, at *best*, if I am making them for a wedding or something I might stack the deck a little with fortunes related to love, relationships, family, that sort of thing. But those," I pointed at the bag again, "those are from back when I made them for restaurants, and I promise you I couldn't tell you which fortunes I sent to which locations back then even if my life depended on it."

I sat back, feeling a little light headed. Fuller for his part simply sat there, motionless and looking straight at me. I could practically feel him reading me, going over the words I had spoken, weighing them up, looking to see if I was being truthful or not. It made me feel distinctly uncomfortable I can tell you and I could only imagine the effect that such an approach would have had on someone who was actually hiding something. But this whole thing was just one big crazy coincidence. I could see why it would be so important to Fuller, why he might read more into it than was there. My cookies really had in all likelihood saved his son's life and that was amazing in its own way. But if he thought there was more to it than that, that I was somehow the Nostradamus of home baking, then he was sorely mistaken. Finally his stern face relaxed into something approaching a reassuring smile and when he spoke his voice was softer and warmer than before. I couldn't help but think he was switching to good cop mode.

"I believe you Mr Lander. I believe you are telling the truth."

I let out a sigh; it looked like this craziness would soon be over.

"Thank you," I said.

Fuller held up a finger, stopping me from saying more.

"Or perhaps more accurately I should say that I believe that you believe what you are saying is true. I also think you're wrong."

I felt my heart drop in my chest and I buried my head into my hands, pressing my palms hard against my eyes. This couldn't be happening. I'd clearly let a crazy man into my house, moreover one that I was sure could do me both physical and legal harm should he want to. I now had no doubt that this had nothing to do with any official police investigation, that he had used his badge and the authority it carried to gain access to my house under false pretences and that, given he believed I was somehow able to tell the future by way of baked goods, he was more than likely a little mentally unstable. I felt a shiver of fear run up my spine and sweat break out on my forehead beneath my fingers. What moments before had felt like a heart-warming story was rapidly turning into a tale of horror as far as I was concerned. I needed to play this carefully.

Get him out as quickly and gently as possible, maybe even consider calling some police officers of my own. I lowered my hands, forced a smile and tried to talk my way out of this.

"Look," I started to say but again Fuller cut me off.

This time he held up a black covered, A5 notebook that I guessed he had taken from a pocket whilst my eyes had been covered. The notebook looked worn and well used, and I could see additional pieces of paper had been slotted between the pages here and there, as well as a couple more of the small evidence bags. I looked at the book and then at Fuller.

"What's that?" I asked, unsure if I actually wanted to know the answer.

Fuller looked at the book and drew it down to his lap and placed his other hand on top of it in an almost reverent way that made me think of vicars with Bibles.

"This," he said, a smile curling up the corner of his lips, "is two years' worth of investigation."

I said nothing and his eyes turned to focus on me again.

"This is every instance I could find where one of your fortunes has turned up at a crime scene in the Greater London area."

His eyes bored into mine and I could tell he was reading me once more.

"This," he continued, "is a record of every life

your fortune cookies have saved, and every death that occurred as a result of your warnings going unheeded."

His smile vanished.

"While I'll accept that you may not be lying to me, this is how I know you are not telling the truth."

4

"A good book can change your outlook on many things."
The Wisdom of Zhu Zhuang, No. 703

I sat there staring at the book on the policeman's lap, doing what I imagined was a pretty good impression of a fish, my mouth opening and closing as I tried and failed to think of something sensible to say in response to Fuller's latest proclamation. Finally I came up with something.

"Right," I said. Eat your heart out Shakespeare.

Fuller chuckled a little at this.

"If you really don't know anything about this Mr Lander I can understand how this could all seem a little strange."

I shook my head.

"No, no, this sort of thing happens to me all the time," I said waving my hand in a dismissive gesture. "Police officers are always turning up at my door with books full of predictions I've made about the future. It's all a little repetitive to be honest, I mean you're the third one this week alone."

Fuller nodded and smiled.

"Fair enough, guess I deserved that."

"You think?" I said, leaning forward a little. "Look, I am really not sure where you are going with this, but to be honest you are starting to creep me out a little. Now I can understand you keeping the fortunes related to your son, I mean I get how they might have had an impact on you and why you would have wanted to hold onto them. But if that book really does contain more of my fortunes that you have picked up from crime scenes all over London, well I hope you won't be offended if I find that a little, oh what's the word, stark raving bonkers."

Fuller chuckled again at this, though his eyes still retained their stony appearance and I couldn't help but wonder if he was putting on this apparent jovial nature as part of his good cop routine. Still, it was better than the simmering anger just shy of the boil that I'd seen flashes of earlier so I decided not to push it. Gift horses and all that.

"Mr Lander, I get that this is all very unusual and

out of the ordinary, I really do. Believe me when I first encountered your fortune cookies and your words saved my son's life I wrote the whole thing off as a coincidence as well. I'd stuck them in my wallet at the restaurant because they'd had such an impact on me, and after that I kind of held onto them as a sort of, I don't know, good luck charm I guess. Plus it made for a good story to tell people, but I really didn't give them much more thought than that."

He tapped his hand on the book again.

"That was until I started to come across them at crime scenes."

I shook my head. This was plain mental as far as I was concerned and I was getting to the point where I didn't really want to hear any more.

"It's only a coincidence," I said, almost pleading with Fuller. "It's like when you learn a new word and you start encountering it everywhere. It's your brain playing tricks on you. The word was there all along but because you didn't know it you simply didn't notice it. Same with my fortune cookies. I bet you've been to plenty of crime scenes where my fortunes didn't make an appearance, and many where they did but you didn't notice because you weren't really aware of them. My fortunes had a major impact on you, heck I'll even grant you that it was something of a miracle, but then they got stuck in your head and when you came across them again you read more into them than was there. I'm sorry, I don't mean to imply that you're nuts or anything, but it is just a coincidence and I think you need to realise that and move on."

Fuller's eyebrows climbed up his forehead again as I stopped talking as if to ask if I was quite finished. I swallowed, aware that I seemed to be making a lot of forceful little speeches tonight. For his part Fuller simply lifted the book and held it out to me.

"Take it," he said.

I looked down at the book and leant away from it.

"I'd rather not," I said suddenly really not wanting to know what was written between the pages of the small black book.

Fuller's eyes grew a few degrees colder.

"Take it," He said again, this time with a trace of iron in his words.

I swallowed again. God, where had this lump in my throat come from? I still didn't believe anything he was saying about my fortunes predicting events, but at the same time I was starting to freak out a little over the implications of a policeman becoming obsessed with my fortune cookies to the point he would collect them in a book and come to confront me with them late on a Friday night. But at the same time I couldn't think of anything else I could reasonably do but indulge him a bit more and hope that it would be enough to satisfy him so that he would leave. So I reached out and took the book. It was heavier than I'd expected, but then I'd not had much experience with books full of crazy so I had nothing to compare it to.

"Open it," Fuller said, "any page."

I looked down at the book, turned it round so that it was the right way up and opened it at around the halfway point. Right there on the left hand page, held in place with a paper clip, was another of my fortunes. This one was considerably more worse for wear than the two Fuller had shown me earlier, the vellum crumpled and stained brown in places. I glanced up at Fuller who nodded his head slightly and so, as I had done before, I read the fortune out loud.

"There is no time like the present to get in shape, walk home tonight, you won't regret it. The Wisdom of Zhu Zhuang, number 830."

I winced slightly. It wasn't one of my best, very generic, and more than likely written close to New Year when lots of people had new gym memberships burning a hole in their pockets. In fact, now that I thought about it, I was probably one of them at the time and I could remember writing several motivational 'get fit' fortunes as much for my own benefit as anyone else's, not that it ended up working, well not for me anyway. Unsure where this was going my eyes drifted over to the right hand page and the newspaper clipping stuck in place with sticky tape. I felt a chill run through me, though exactly what aspect of the whole thing caused it I couldn't say. Again I read out loud.

"Man dies in late night bus crash."

I looked up at Fuller.

"What the hell is this?" I demanded.

Fuller gestured at the fortune on the left hand page.

"They took that out of the pocket of the victim," he said matter-of-factly. "He was coming home from an evening out with friends, a meal at a Chinese restaurant in Camden. He was only about a half hours walk from home, but he decided to take the bus instead."

"And what? What are you saying? That if he'd done what the fortune said and had walked home, he wouldn't have died?"

"It seems fairly obvious to me that that's the case. If he didn't get on the bus he wouldn't have been in the accident."

I clenched my jaw at this, restricting myself to only thinking 'no shit Sherlock' rather than actually saying it.

"And if he had decided to walk," I said instead, "and he got hit by a car, would you have included the story in your little book? Or do you just cherry pick the stories that fit?"

Fuller didn't grace this with a reply. Instead he nodded towards the book in my hands.

"Pick another page," he said in a tone that made it clear I didn't really have a choice in the matter.

I did as he said, flipping through a few pages and

stopping at one close to the front of the book. The first thing that caught my eye this time was a police mug shot of a white man in his mid to late twenties. He was handsome in a way that I found slightly annoying, with hair styled into a quiff and shaven short at the sides. He was also sporting a black eye and a bloody lip that somewhat marred his boy band heart throb appearance, and there was a look of darkest hate in his eyes. I was immediately struck by the thought that this man was a predator, using his looks to draw in the unwary. I lifted the photo to look at the piece of paper held in place beneath and found myself reading the rap sheet of one Tyler Hunter Morgan, which was perhaps the most millennial name I had ever heard. I quickly found that my initial assessment of Mr T.H. Morgan had been on the money. He had a string of minor charges to his name, including a couple of drunk and disorderly arrests and an antisocial behaviour order, as well as, most recently, a conviction for attempted sexual assault.

On the other page was another photograph of someone who was the polar opposite of Tyler. The woman was around the same age, probably a few years older but with an innocence to her smile that somehow made her seem younger. She had shoulder length mousy brown hair and was wearing a green knitted sweater that looked either homemade or second hand. Everything about her screamed Primary School teacher to me and I was actually surprised when I looked at the piece of paper below the photo to find that Emma Billing actually worked in a bank. Unlike Tyler I liked her immediately, since whereas his photo radiated narcissistic entitlement Emma's seemed to depict a warm, genuine person the kind of which there are sadly too few of in the world.

The fortune was once again attached to the book with a paperclip, this time secured to the bottom right corner of the page baring Emma's photo and details. I read it through in my head and felt my brow crinkle in confusion. I looked back at the two photos again. There was something of an obvious story there, one I was pretty sure I wasn't going to like that much, but to which the fortune simply didn't seem to apply. With the bus crash I could see the connection right away, even if I found it decidedly tenuous, but this time round I was at a complete loss.

"It is never too late for a touch of spring cleaning and a fresh start to life. The Wisdom of Zhu Zhuang, number 151."

I looked up at Fuller.

"I don't get it," I said. "How does my fortune relate to these two people?"

Fuller leant forward, twisting his head slightly so that he could get a better look at the pages open before me.

"Ah yes, Tyler Morgan, nasty little shit," his eyes flicked to mine and he held up a hand. "Please excuse my language."

I said it was fine and asked him to continue. Fuller sat back again and crossed his arms across his chest as he spoke.

"Tyler is one of those people who thinks his good looks and his family's money can get him out of whatever trouble he gets himself into. And sadly, for the most part he was right. You saw his criminal record, well that's only a fraction of the things he got up to, only the things we could make stick. He carried out at least three other sexual assaults that we know of, and I can tell you that once he had finished with them the women didn't look half as pretty as Emma there. But every time he walked, always had an alibi for the time of the attacks, and his father's fancy lawyers always found a way to dismiss any forensic evidence collected."

Fuller snorted.

"You see Tyler had an MO, he would target groups of girls on a night out, never approach an individual on her own. Then he would single out the quiet one, the girl that seemed shy and uncomfortable, like she didn't really want to be there. He'd turn on the charm, make her feel relaxed, be the perfect gentleman, always making sure she felt comfortable and safe surrounded by her friends. And after that, at the end of the evening, he would help the girl into her coat and offer her a friendly hug. And right there your honour is the reason my client's DNA was found at the crime scene."

Fuller bared his teeth for a moment.

"He's a shit, but he's a smart one."

He took a deep breath.

"Anyway, he'd follow his chosen lady home and if he saw the chance he'd break into her house and, well I will spare you the details. It wasn't rape if that's what you're thinking, not definitionally anyway, but it wasn't far off it. But like I said we could never prove anything. He would wear a mask and gloves you see, and always had his mates handy to provide an alibi if needed and that clever little trick of his to explain away any DNA he might have left behind."

I shook my head.

"That's awful, but I still don't get what that has to do with the fortune."

Fuller nodded.

"As I am sure you can guess Tyler targeted Emma Billing, met her on a Saturday night when she was out with her work friends celebrating a colleague's birthday. He apparently made an impression on her and they hit it off well, even exchanged numbers. And of course at the end of the night he helped her into her coat and gave her a hug, even a kiss on the cheek."

Fuller's top lip curled up in disgust.

"And afterwards he followed her home and around two thirty in the morning he broke into her house."

I felt a chill pass through me.

"Oh god, did he hurt her?" I asked, not really wanting to know the answer.

Fuller smiled and shook his head.

"No, she was perfectly fine, though I can't say the same for Tyler."

"What happened?"

Fuller chuckled.

"What happened is that the night before she ordered a Chinese takeaway. She got her hands on one of your fortunes, and she did what it said."

My look was clearly as blank as my understanding as Fuller shifted on the sofa, scooting to the edge and leaning slightly towards me.

"Ok, so you see at the time Emma was living in this little two-bedroom, Victorian era terraced house that she inherited from an aunt when she died. When Tyler broke in, she had been there for the best part of five years, and the place was still full of her aunt's old stuff. Anyway, the night before she reads your fortune and decides that, finally, she has to do something about it. So on that Saturday she sets about sorting out all her aunt's stuff and boxing it up to give to charity. Well the job proved more than she had bargained for and she was far from done by the time she had to get ready to go out that evening. There was stuff everywhere, every inch of the place covered in some manner of junk or another."

He smiled as if he were telling a joke and was anticipating the punchline.

"So Emma gets home from her night out, picks her way through the mess and heads to bed vowing to finish it off in the morning. Middle of the night she gets woken up by cry followed by a loud crash coming from right outside her door. She looks out and what do you think she finds?"

"Tyler," I said.

"Tyler," Fuller confirmed with the widest smile yet. "The little creep had broken in, got all the way up the stairs without waking Emma, only to get his feet tangled up in a pile of Emma's aunt's old clothes, lose his balance, fall back down the stairs, slamming head first into the wall and knocking himself out cold."

He chuckled again clearly enjoying the sex pest's comeuppance.

"By the time the police arrived he was starting to come round. There he was, laying there at the bottom the stairs, balaclava over his head, gloves on his hands, cable ties and, well, other stuff that I will again spare you the details of in a bag still slung over his shoulder. No way was he talking himself out of that one. And what's more they found evidence connecting him to other assaults in the bag as well. He was well and truly stitched up."

He gestured to the book.

"At the time I printed out his rap sheet he'd only been convicted for the attempted attack on Emma, but he ended up going down for the other three as well. He's gonna be inside for a long time yet, and from what I hear karma can be a real pain in the arse."

I winced at the implication, but I couldn't bring myself to feel sorry for Tyler in any way. He was getting what he deserved as far as I was concerned. We sat in silence for a few moments, me thinking over what Fuller had said and adding it to the previous story about the bus accident, and Fuller watching me intently, waiting for me to come to the same conclusion he had already reached. But unfortunately for him I wasn't quite there yet.

"I'm not sure what you want me to say, well ok I am, but I am not sure I can say it. If all this is true then it's weird, it really is, and I don't have a good explanation for it at all. But I'm sorry, I am not ready to accept that, quote, I have magic powers that I am completely unaware of and which manifest themselves through the medium of novelty fortune cookies, end quote, is the answer here."

Fuller's shoulders slumped ever so slightly. He looked over at the clock above my fireplace, then pulled back his sleeve and checked his watch as if unwilling to trust the time keeping apparatus of someone so unwilling to see what was apparently blatantly obvious to him.

"It's late," he said, finally arriving at the conclusion I'd reached when he first rang my doorbell. "We should pick this up in the morning."

I was tempted to argue but I seriously doubted I would get far with that approach. I closed the book and held it out to him. He looked at it for a moment before shaking his head.

"No, you keep it, at least for now. Read through it and we can talk about it tomorrow."

He reached into his inside jacket pocket and pulled out a business card and a biro. He flipped the card over and scribbled something on the back.

"I'm staying in the village for the night. Here's my mobile number in case you need to call me," he handed me the card. "I'll be going to the All-Day Café for breakfast, do you know it?"

I told him I did.

"Good, I'll see you there at 8:30."

I was tempted to protest his assumption that I would be joining him, but I quickly dismissed the idea. If I didn't turn up chances were good he would just turn up at my house again, and all things considered I'd be happier dealing with him on neutral ground. Fuller stood in one quick, forceful movement and held out his hand. I fumbled the book into my left hand, stood awkwardly, and shook the offered appendage.

"Read the book," he said in a voice that made it clear he would not be pleased if I skimped on this particular homework assignment.

I nodded and said that I would. He looked at me for a moment before nodding, apparently happy with whatever he had read from me.

"I was wrong to assume you knew what was going on here," he said in a way that made me think he didn't admit to mistakes that often. "It made sense to me that you would, but now that I've met you I believe that you are as in the dark about all this as I was a couple of years back. But once you've read the book maybe it will all start to make sense to you."

He turned and headed quickly towards the door. I followed, opened the door, we said our goodbyes and he was gone, absorbed back into the dark, drizzly night from which he had come. I closed the door and walked slowly back into my living room, lost in my own thoughts. I sat down, reached out and picked up my hot chocolate and took an absent-minded sip, and immediately spat it back into the mug. It was stone cold of course and tasted decidedly unpleasant. I put the mug down and turned my attention to the book I was still holding in my left hand.

"This is insane," I said out loud, because talking to yourself like that is the height of sanity.

And then I opened the book and started to read.

5

"A good meal will help set you on the right path for the day."
The Wisdom of Zhu Zhuang, No. 21

I didn't sleep that night.

I know, shocking. I mean usually you would expect to sleep like a baby the night after a large, intimidating police officer turns up at your house and presents you will a book full of strange, disturbing, and often violent events that you supposedly have some kind of supernatural connection to. Better than counting sheep I hear. But no, instead I'd lain awake for hours on end, going over and over everything Fuller had said, trying to find some way to make sense of what he had told me and what was written in the book that didn't involve me being an unwitting psychic. Like I said, no one could have seen my sleepless night coming.

To be clear I still didn't believe that the conclusion Fuller had reached was the correct one. There had to be a more rational explanation for what was going on than precognitive baking, and preferably one that didn't violate the laws of causality, or the laws of physics for that matter. But try as I might nothing was coming to mind, and there are only so many times you can claim something is a coincidence before you start to doubt it yourself.

The book that Fuller had left me contained thirty-seven events in which my fortunes appeared to have played some kind of role. Some of them, much like the incident with the bus crash, were fairly easy to connect. The person in question had received one of my fortunes that told them, in my usual open-ended way, to do or not do something; they ignored it and soon after became a police statistic. Individually they could be easily written off as someone wanting to see something that wasn't really there, but together they painted a disturbingly compelling picture. The majority of the entries however had more in common with the events surrounding Tyler and his attempted assault of Emma Billing. There was some information about a crime that was either thwarted or seen to fruition, attached to which was one of my fortunes that, lacking the crucial contextual information, I just couldn't connect to the events described. But Fuller had, and I was in little doubt that once he explained the various events to me, I would be able to see the connection as well, regardless of how much I might not want to.

But if I am honest what kept me awake the most was the paradigm shifting possibility that Fuller might be right, and if he was what on earth that could mean. If I really was able to predict the future and pass that information onto people via my fortune cookies did that give me some kind of responsibility to continue doing so? If one day I decided to hang it up and get a different, less unusual, hobby would that result in a slew of crimes and accidents that would have otherwise been prevented from taking place? And how on earth was I meant to sit down and casually write fortunes now when the spectre of possible disaster, death, and destruction hung over every stylised word I wrote. Heck, even the slim chance that it could all be true made me never want to pick up pen and ink again, but the idea of not doing so made me feel immediately guilty, as if I would be in some way directly responsible for the actions of the next Tyler Hunter Morgan to stalk the nightclubs of London.

I moved through my morning routine in a daze, not really focusing on anything I was doing. I got up, let Bob out into the garden, emptied Tortoise's litter tray and fed them both. I then stood in the shower for a long time, letting the water run down over my head and wondering whether there was a Nobel prize for demonstrating that psychic powers existed. I was pretty sure someone offered money for that sort of thing at the very least. I finally roused myself enough to actually get washed when the water started to run cold, only to find I had left my bath towel on my bed and had to dry myself the best I could using a hand towel instead. I dressed in pretty much the same clothes I had been wearing the night before, save for fresh socks and underwear of course, and headed to the kitchen for a cup of tea. I was about to pour myself a bowl of cereal when I remembered I was meant to be meeting Fuller for breakfast. I looked at the kitchen clock and was surprised to see it had already gone 8. I really was out of sorts today, by this time in the morning I would usually be halfway through taking Bob for his morning walk. I went out into the hall to find Bob sitting there facing the door, his nose inches from its wooden surface. He turned as I approached and gave me a dismissive sideways look, though his tail started to wag furiously.

"Giving mixed signals there buddy," I said, giving his head a quick scratch.

Bob hopped up onto his feet and I attached his lead to his collar, pulled on my coat and was about to open the door when I remembered Fuller's book was still sitting on my bedside table. I dropped his lead and hurried to the bedroom, grabbed the book and headed back downstairs to find that Bob had regained his sitting position in front of the door, only this time his nose was actually touching it. Point taken. I opened the door and Bob immediately forgave me my trespasses and bounded outside, tongue lolling and the entire back half of his body moving back and forth with excitement.

It took the best part of twenty minutes to walking into town and as such by the time I arrived outside the All-Day Café I was already late for my meeting with Fuller. I could see the police officer sitting inside and, as if possessing psychic powers of his own, he seemed to sense me looking at him and turned to face me. I gave a small wave and he nodded back in reply.

"Ok, you wait here," I said to Bob, tying his lead to a post placed there for that very purpose. "If you behave, I'll bring you back a sausage."

Bob's ears pricked up at this, demonstrating once again that he did understand what I was saying, he just chose to ignore me most of the time. Clearly he had been spending too much time with my cat. I opened the door to the café and headed across the small room and pulled up a chair across from Fuller. The All-Day Café was everything you would expect it to be. There were a dozen plastic topped tables crammed into the place, eight of which were four seaters while the rest only provided seating for two. The right hand wall was tiled wood, while the left hand side sported bare brick. The walls were hung with framed photographs of the local area taken by the owners, there was a notice board overflowing with flyers for local events, goods, and services, and of course the obligatory large flat screen TV playing Sky News on mute taking up pride of place beside the counter.

Despite there only being two of us at this little meeting Fuller had selected one of the four seater tables. He had also decided not to bother waiting for me to arrive before ordering food and was already tucking into his breakfast of beans, sausages, bacon, mushrooms, hash browns, toast and a poached egg with relish, that's the emotion not the condiment. A large mug of steaming hot tea sat beside him completing the whole appetising arrangement and my stomach grumbled audibly as I sat down.

"Good morning Mr Lander," he said, a fully loaded fork halfway between his plate and mouth.

"Detective Fuller."

Fuller looked at me in silence for a moment and, with a soft snort and a nod of his head, put down his fork and reached his hand across the table.

"Please, call me Peter," he said. "Given the situation I think we can do away with formalities, don't you?"

I shook the offered hand.

"Steve," I said, even though he already knew that. "And thanks for the sleepless night."

It was at that moment I noticed the waitress had approached silently and was now standing beside our table and when I looked up at her there was a wry smile at the corner of her lips.

"Can I get you anything love?" she asked in the time-honoured manner of café waitresses nationwide.

"Umm, I'll have what he's got," I said.

"No doubt," the waitress said with a wink, before heading off to the kitchen to deliver my order and leaving my cheeks burning a little.

"So," said Peter, "you read the book then."

I nodded.

"And?" he asked.

I'd known he would ask this before I'd even left the house, there was no way he couldn't, and yet I still wasn't sure how to answer. I wasn't ready to commit to 'psychic powers are real' just yet, but neither could I simply dismiss the whole thing. Instead I shrugged and went for honesty.

"I have no idea whatsoever," I said.

Peter chuckled around a mouthful of beans.

"I looked at all the cases in your book," I continued, "and though a lot of them made no sense to me the ones that did, I will admit, appear to be, somewhat, related to my fortunes, in a roundabout fashion."

Peter looked me in the eye.

"Would you like to add any more qualifiers to that sentence?" he asked.

"Sorry, look, there is something here, something I don't understand, something that seems to defy what I would expect from coincidence and probability alone, I will grant all of that. But I can't believe that the only explanation available is that I have psychic powers that I don't know anything about. That, to me, seems even crazier than the idea that psychic powers are real in the first place."

Peter pursed his thin lips slightly and nodded.

"I've been thinking about that," he said. "I did a lot of reading when I first started believing that there was something genuinely unusual about your fortune cookies. I wanted to try and work out how someone could possibly know the things written in the fortunes before they took place. I pretty much came to the conclusion that you had to either be some sort of super villain of Machiavellian proportions, or you were psychic."

I swallowed.

"Hopefully you've ruled out the first one at least," I said with a nervous laugh.

Peter's eyes turned on me again and once more I got the sense he was reading me. He smiled.

"Unless I am getting you completely wrong, and I don't think I am, then I don't think I have to worry about that. You seem an honest sort to me."

"Ah," I said holding up a finger, "which is exactly what a Machiavellian super villain would want you to think."

Peter looked at me and said nothing.

"Sorry," I said, and lowered my finger.

"Anyway, after meeting you last night I also

decided that you were telling the truth about having no knowledge of what was going on with your fortunes. So, I decided to rule out the idea that you are a psychic as well, or at least not in the conventional sense anyway."

I raised my eyebrows at this.

"There's a conventional way to have psychic powers?"

"Sure there is, the whole Sally Morgan, Derek Acorah sort of thing. Getting voices from the other side, passing messages on from the dearly departed to the recently bereaved. The whole crystal ball, tarot card, palm reading lot. You know the type."

I did, I'd seen Most Haunted. Don't hold it against me.

"But you don't think that's what I am then?"

He shook his head again and started mopping up his now empty plate with his last piece of toast.

"No, not any more anyway."

"But," I said, "you do still think I am some sort of psychic?"

Peter nodded and held up a finger to request I give him a moment as he swallowed down a mouthful of toast.

"Have you ever heard of automatic writing?"

"Is that the thing that produces Daily Mail headlines?"

Peter chuckled.

"No, but I can see how you can make that mistake. No, automatic writing is a form of psychic ability where someone writes something but the source of the words comes from something other than their conscious mind."

"Like what?"

Peter shrugged.

"It could just be the subconscious mind, but generally it is believed to come from some external source of supernatural or spiritual origin."

"Right," I said, "so ghost dictation? You think that voices from the great beyond are telling me what to write in such a way that I am completely unaware of it?"

Peter shrugged again and lined his knife and fork up on his now empty plate. He picked up a napkin and dabbed at the corners of his mouth.

"Look, I know how it sounds, but, if you think about it, it fits with what we know."

"Which is what exactly?"

"Well, we know that on numerous occasions your fortunes appeared to have had a profound effect on people's lives in a manner that doesn't seem readily explicable. We also know that you claim to have no idea how they are doing so."

I opened my mouth to protest the implication that I might still not be telling the truth but Peter cut me off.

"Something I am completely willing to accept," he said.

I shut my mouth again. Peter continued.

"So if we assume that the source of the

apparently precognitive information contained in your fortunes is not coming directly from you, well, that means it must be coming from somewhere else, something beyond you. To me that suggests automatic writing or possibly some kind of possession I guess."

"Right," I said, "so either way you think someone has been using my body for their own ends without me knowing about it?"

The waitress placed my breakfast down in front of me and I looked up to see that wry smile again, her pencilled eyebrows high on her forehead.

"We should all be so lucky," she said with another wink.

I started impersonating a fish again and could feel the heat growing in my cheeks once more.

"Can I get you anything else or are you all set?"

"Umm, no, I'm good thanks, all good," I sputtered.

"Wonderful," she said "I'll leave you two to your adventures."

She turned and walked over to the counter where she immediately started whispering to another waitress who joined her in shooting furtive glances our way.

"Well, I can never show my face here again," I said.

Peter shook his head.

"If the worse you have to worry about is a couple of bored waitresses thinking you have a more interesting sex life than you do then I think you are doing pretty well."

I decided to focus on adding milk and sugar to my mug of tea rather than responding to that. I took a sip and attempted to carry on as if the last few seconds had never happened.

"So, automatic writing, how's that meant to work?"

"Well, as I understand it, there's a receiver, that would be you."

I almost choked on some sausage at this. Ironic I know.

"Anyway," Peter continued with a slight shake of his head, "the idea is that you go somewhere nice and quiet, put yourself in a relaxed state, deep breaths and all that, and try to clear your mind and write down whatever comes to you, without really focusing on what you are putting down. Any of that sound familiar?"

I swallowed down a mouthful of egg. It did sound familiar, very familiar in fact. I had something of a ritual when it came to coming up with my fortunes. I would always do it at the end of the day, after I'd fed my animals and eaten myself. I would go up to my craft room, turn on only the table lamp, put on a bit of soft music, and make myself comfortable at my craft table. I'd pull out a fresh sheet of A4 paper, pick up a pencil and close my eyes, try to clear my mind of any distracting thoughts, and wait for an idea to come to me. As soon as one did I would quickly write it down before closing my eyes again and attempting to push what I had just written completely from my mind. I'd do this until I had a dozen or so rough ideas scribbled down on the paper and then I'd go through, edit out the ones that seemed a bit crap or simply made no sense, after which I would actively work to come up with as many different versions of each of the remaining fortunes as I could think of. This way I would end up with a hundred or so new fortunes for my cookies from a little over an hour's work. The actual transferring of the fortunes to vellum and the baking of the cookies themselves would happen on another day during daylight hours.

"Yeah," I said my voice catching a bit, "that all sounds about right."

Peter's eyebrows shot up at this.

"Really? You really think it's possible that you could be engaging in automatic writing when you write your fortunes without realising it?"

I didn't reply straight away. The whole idea of someone or something putting ideas into my head made me uncomfortable. Not to mention the fact that I rather prided myself on my fortunes, but if what Peter was saying was correct then could I really claim to have been responsible for any of them? Was I not only a psychic without knowing it, but a plagiarist as well? With all this running through my head I finally nodded.

"I'm not saying that I think you are right, but yeah, if that's how automatic writing is meant to work then, sure, it sounds like I might be doing it."

He smiled a warm, genuine smile that seemed wholly different from anything I had seen from him so far.

"Wow, this is great, this feels like progress."

"Glad I can be of help," I said, before popping a piece of bacon into my mouth.

His eyes locked onto me at this.

"The question is, would you be willing to help me some more?" he asked.

Again I didn't reply straight away. Instead I took a sip of tea and weighed up the options. Option one, I said no, took Bob home and tried to put the whole strange encounter out of my mind. And then what? Would I be able to carry on making fortune cookies as before? I didn't see how that would be possible with the ideas Peter had planted in my head. Even if everything he had said about my fortunes being prophetic was wrong I couldn't imagine being able to write them in the same relaxed way again. I would be constantly editing myself, over thinking every word I came up with, looking for hidden meaning in every cleverly worded instruction to lose weight and get more exercise. The quality of my fortunes would undoubtedly suffer as a result and being the perfectionist I am that would simply drive me crazy. So would I give it up instead? Stop making fortune cookies and take up tapestry making or something, and spend the rest of my life wondering if I was in some way responsible for every terrible thing I saw on the nightly news? That didn't seem like fun either. All of which brought me to option two, which was to head down the rabbit hole and see where it led me.

"Why is it that I suddenly feel like I'm standing on the banks of the Rubicon?"

Peter inclined his head slightly.

"Maybe you are," he said.

I chuckled to myself at this. This was all crazy, but could I really turn my back on it and carry on as if nothing had happened? I didn't think I could. I drained the rest of my tea and put the mug down a little more forcefully than intended.

"Ok," I said before I could change my mind, "where do we go from here."

Peter smiled and reached down and picked up a Tesco's carrier bag, one of the tatty old ones from before they started charging you for them, and placed it on the table.

"What's that?" I asked.

Peter said nothing. Instead he turned the bag over and with obvious care emptied the content out onto the table. I stared at the objects on the table and knew I was doing the fish thing again with my mouth. Laid out before me, bundled up neatly in their beeswax origami wrapping paper and secured with a red satin bow, were eight of my fortune cookies, unopened and pristine.

"We," said Peter, looking me in the eye once more, "start here."

6

"Listen to stories from the past, they can point the way."
The Wisdom of Zhu Zhuang, No. 931

I sat there, a fork full of baked beans inches from my mouth, staring at the eight fortune cookies scattered haphazardly across the plastic top of the All-Day Café table. Judging from the slight differences in the design of the packaging these cookies represented examples of my work spanning at least a four, maybe even a five year period, longer than the amount of time that Peter had told me he had been aware of them. I put my fork down, still fully loaded, and reached out and picked up one of the cookies. This one looked distinctly different from the rest, with the satin ribbon being wrapped around it in such a way as to form a cross beneath the bow, much like you would see on fake Christmas presents in the window of big department stores.

"Where did you get this?" I asked, holding up the cookie. "This is one of my earliest designs; I haven't made them like this in years."

"You'd be surprised the things people hold onto," Peter said by way of an answer. "Like I said before, your fortune cookies are little works of art in their own right; it seems a fair number of people chose to hold onto them as is rather than actually opening them."

I looked at the wrapped cookie held delicately in my fingers trying to estimate exactly when it had been created. No more than six months after Laci had died would be my guess, back when I was still throwing myself into my hobby to an obsessive level as a way to avoid other people and my own feelings. I felt a catch in my throat. This cookie, wrapped up in bright coloured beeswax paper and tied with a happy little bow, was a physical representation of my grief. I put it back down quickly as I felt my emotions start to boil up beneath the surface.

"I came across that one when investigating an attempted robbery a little over a year ago. It was sitting on the mantelpiece, sandwiched between pictures of grinning grandchildren and a collection of porcelain pigs. I of course recognised it straight away so I asked if I could take it, explained that it might help with another enquiry I was pursuing."

I gave him a look.

"What?" he said, with a shrug. "It wasn't a lie; I never stated it was an official police investigation. Anyway, they let me have it. I only had two others in my collection at that point, the rest I have picked up at various places across London since then, the most recent only the other week."

"Ok," I said still feeling in the dark as to what exactly was going on here, "what do we do next?"

Peter shifted in his chair slightly as though, now that it came to it, he wasn't entirely confident in his own plan.

"Well, to my way of thinking, if there really is something special about your fortune cookies, if they really can foretell the future in some way, it makes sense to me that we start with them."

"By which you mean?"

He shrugged again, a gesture of his I was starting to recognise.

"I mean we open one of them, see what it says."

I looked down at the cookies and then back up at Peter.

"Just open one of them?"

"Yeah."

"At random?"

"Yeah."

"Right," I said.

I looked at the cookies once more.

"So, umm, do you want to do the honours?"

Peter shook his head.

"I think it should be you, that way I can't be said to be influencing the course of the investigation."

I gave him a look. He turned his eyes away from mine.

"Alright, I don't know what it is, but, well, it feels wrong for me to do it," he shifted in his chair again. "I can't explain it, but it's like I've already had my turn, you know what I mean? When I read the fortune that saved my son's life it was like that was it, that was my one spin of the wheel. Like tempting fate, that sort of thing. I've had my answer; it's your turn now."

I looked at the cookies once more.

"But there are eight of them," I said.

Peter shrugged.

"Maybe some people take a little bit longer to get the message than others, or maybe it works differently because you're the one who made them. I don't know, I don't make the rules. All I know is that if you don't open one of them I'm not going to. It ends here."

I met Peter's gaze and could tell at once that he was serious about this. He had followed this strange investigation for two years now, but I could tell he was being truthful about packing the whole thing in if I didn't open one of the cookies. I considered for a moment that maybe that would be the best thing for both of us, but then, before I could dwell on that idea, I reached out and picked up the cookie I had been holding earlier once more.

"It's been long enough," I said, unsure if I was talking to Peter, myself, or the cookie.

With more delicacy than was necessary I carefully undid the bow and slid the satin ribbon off of the beeswax cover and placed it on the table. It struck me that I had never actually opened one of my fortune cookies before. Sure, I always ate one or two of each batch I made to make sure they tasted right, but once they were all wrapped up I'd always felt as though my ownership of them had ended, and that somehow they already belonged to whomever it would be that would end up opening them. It would have been wrong to open a gift intended for someone else. Moving my hands as slowly and deftly as I did when I wrapped them I opened the beeswax sheet and lifted the cookie from its folds.

I was surprised to see that it was still in remarkably good condition for something baked almost half a decade ago. I was even more surprised when I broke it in half and it still let out the distinct crack I knew all too well. If I hadn't known better I could have easily mistaken it for a cookie baked fresh that morning. I placed one half of the cookie onto the beeswax wrapping and, using thumb and forefinger, extracted the fortune from the remaining piece, which I placed beside its twin. Just like the cookie itself the vellum seemed to have weathered the years incredibly well and looked as fresh as the day I'd cut it. The material was of course of the older stock that I no longer used, and when I turned it over and saw the calligraphy itself I could tell at once exactly what ink I have used and which pen I had used to write the message.

"What does it say?" asked Peter, making me jump slightly.

I looked up to see him leaning forward trying to read the message upside-down. I had a sudden childish impulse to hide it from him, as if the information it contained was somehow secret and meant for my eyes only, but I pushed it quickly away. I cleared my throat and read.

"It says, when starting out on a journey it always pays to start at the beginning of the story. The Wisdom of Zhu Zhuang number sixty seven."

I met Peter's eye.

"What does it mean?" I asked.

He shrugged.

"No idea, you made it, you tell me."

I looked back down at the short message. Of course I knew what it actually meant, which was very little. It came from a time when I was trying a bit too hard to sound strange and mysterious. I had just started actively selling the cookies rather than only making them for people I knew, having added in the Zhu Zhuang persona as part of the marketing, and I was still in the process of finding my own style. Instead of writing what felt natural to me I would do my best to make them sound like every other fortune cookie you might encounter, by which I mean vague, meaningless, pseudo philosophical and with only the illusion of depth. I was about to tell Peter this when a thought occurred to me. I put the fortune down and reached into the pocket of my jacket and pulled out Peter's book. I placed it on the table, opened it to the first page and turned it round to face the detective.

"Maybe it means we should start here?"

The first page of Peter's book held a newspaper clipping, a local colour piece from a copy of the free Metro newspaper dating back a couple of years. It was the only story in the entire book that both didn't come directly from a crime scene and didn't actually have an attached fortune. In fact there was nothing to directly connect it to one of my fortunes, but I could clearly see why Peter had included it, and why it might have prompted him to start collecting details on cases that seemed to involve my cookies.

"Psychic Inception," Peter said reading the headline, "man claims psychic saved his life, psychic claims it was a fortune cookie."

I'd read the story the night before and could remember the basic details included in the few short paragraphs of copy that the editors had allocated to the tale. Daniel Phillips, a forty-seven year old corner shop owner in Southwark, London had visited a tarot card reader who went by the name Madam Josephine, but whose real name was the rather less mystical Rachel Jones. During the reading Madam Josephine had given him the somewhat cryptic advice to avoid the sweetest of gifts, even those coming from a trusted friend. The message had been so at odds with the generalities he had received during the rest of the reading that it had really stuck with him, so much so that he had still been playing it over in his head when, that weekend, he attended a house warming party thrown by his friend, one Thomas Jenkins, whom he had known since Primary School.

The article was heavy on the description and it was easy to picture the scene. Daniel arrived at his friend's new house a little after 7pm and Thomas greeted him at the door, laden down with a tray of double chocolate cupcakes. Daniel, as Thomas well knew, was a big fan of such things, but unfortunately also suffered from a severe peanut allergy that kept him from indulging his sweet tooth too often. However, this too was something that Thomas knew and he assured Daniel that not a single thing his wife, Sandra, had prepared for the party had so much as seen a peanut, let alone actually contained one. His concerns allayed Daniel reached for the cupcakes, apparently 'drooling with desire' if the article was to be believed, when suddenly the words of Madam Josephine popped into his head once more. And so, with great reluctance, Daniel declined the offer.

A few minutes later Sandra noticed the two of them talking and the tray of cupcakes still held in her husband's hands. In a near panic she rushed over, tore the tray from Thomas's grasp, and held it as far away from Daniel as it was physically possible for her to do without actually moving away from him. Breathlessly she explained that the cupcakes, unlike every other piece of food at the party, had not been made by her, but rather had been a gift from their new neighbours. This meant that rather than being able to guarantee that they didn't contain peanuts instead she knew for a fact that they did, with a large spoonful of peanut butter sitting in the deadly heart of every last one of the edible instruments of death. With a start Daniel realised that, in his haste to make it to the party on time, he had forgotten to pick up his EpiPen before leaving the house. Given the severity of his condition a single bite of one of the cupcakes would have killed him long before an ambulance could have arrived with a replacement.

As soon as the immediate shock of his close call passed Daniel started telling anyone who would listen about the cause of his salvation. He insisted that the only reason he was standing there alive at all was the incredible psychic powers of Madam Josephine, tarot card reader extraordinaire and part time sales assistant at Aurora Books, leading purveyor of occult books and paraphernalia in the Greater London area, or at least south of the river anyway. The reporter assigned to the story had dutifully tracked down Madam Josephine, who, in what had to be a rare moment of complete honesty for someone in her profession, had admitted that her advice to Daniel had nothing to do with her psychic powers nor was it anything that she read in the cards, but was rather second hand information that came from a fancy fortune cookie she had received the night before when out on a less than memorable blind date at a Chinese restaurant. The reporter had clearly loved this idea and had played up the Inception style link of a fortune within a fortune, and had been granted a couple of inches of space on page 14 for his troubles, below the fold of course.

"So," I said after giving Peter a few moments to read the short story, "what do you think?"

"Hmm, interesting," he said.

I waiting for him to say more but he was not forth coming.

"So, what does that mean? Do you think we should go to speak to this Daniel Phillips? Is that what the fortune cookie is guiding us to do?"

Even as I said that last bit I felt foolish, but in for a penny and all that. Peter shook his head.

"No, I don't think so."

"Well then what?" I asked. "It was your idea to open one of the cookies and use it as a guide; well, if we assume for a moment that you are right about all this, then as far as I can see it is pointing to that story in your book. If not that then I have no idea what it means."

Peter looked up from the newspaper clipping.

"You misunderstand me. I think you're right that the fortune was pointing to this article, I just don't think we need to go speak to Mr Phillips."

"Well what should we do?" I asked, slightly lost.

Peter tapped a thick finger on the article, indicating a name.

"I think we should go speak to her, we should speak to Madam Josephine."

This took me back a bit, as far as I could see the message in the cookie had, if you accepted the whole supernatural process apparently at play here, clearly been meant for Daniel. Without it he probably would be dead now, probably having expired due to anaphylactic shock right there on Thomas and Sandra's new living room carpet. And while the message had taken an even more circuitous route than normal to reach him in my opinion Madam Josephine was the messenger and nothing more.

"I don't get it, why her and not Daniel? Surely he's the one we should be talking to here."

Peter shook his head.

"Think about it. In every single other case in the book, as well as my own experience, the message in the cookie changed the life, one way or another, of the person who opened it. Well Mr Phillips didn't open the cookie, Madam Josephine did. Sure, the message saved his life, but I don't think it was meant for him, I think it was meant for her, it was meant to change her life in some way."

"What are you saying?" I asked, still not getting it. "That the cookie did a twofer? It saved Daniel's life and did something for Madam Josephine that we don't know about as well?"

Peter shrugged.

"Maybe, or maybe the change hasn't happened for her yet. Maybe all it did at the time was catch the attention of a police officer who was starting to wonder, for the first time in his life, if there could be more to the world than what science has to tell us. Maybe for Madam Josephine the change in her life will take place when that aforementioned police officer and a semi reclusive home baker pay her a visit."

I looked at him in silence, unsure how to respond to that, and admittedly having lost the path of his thinking a little. Peter smiled.

"Eat up," he said gesturing at my half-eaten breakfast. "We're going on a road trip."

7

"A journey taken on trust can yield the most unexpected of results."
The Wisdom of Zhu Zhuang, No. 1241

We dropped Bob back at my house. My shaggy old dog was in high spirits. Not only had he ridden in a car, but, as promised, I had also saved him a sausage from my breakfast. He now would more than likely settle down for a nap in front of the fireplace and consider this a very good day indeed. Before we headed off for London I nipped up to my office and picked up my battered leather messengers bag and, after a moments consideration, plucked an A4 black and red, casebound Oxford notebook from a shelf beside my craft desk and stuffed it into the bag. If you'd asked me I couldn't have explained why I decided to bring it, I just had a feeling that it would come in handy, and given the whole motivation for the journey I was about to embark on I was more willing than usual to listen to the random thoughts and feelings floating around inside my head.

I hurried back down to where Peter was waiting for me, pausing only to give Tortoise a quick scratch under the chin, and climbed into the passenger seat of his dark blue Ford Focus that had clearly seen better days. Peter pealed out of my driveway faster than I would have liked, sending up a spray of gravel in his wake, and we were on our way to London. As I had expected Peter was an aggressive driver, but after the first few miles where I constantly tried to jam my right foot through the floor at every corner we came to I started to relax a bit when I realised that he was undoubtedly in full control of his vehicle and had probably received more driving instruction than most of the other people on the road. That said there were a couple of occasions after that when I found myself reaching for the grab handle on a particularly sharp corner or abrupt stop.

The sky was grey and full of heavy, one might even say portentous, clouds through which the sun was struggling to make its presence known. We passed rolling green fields, many scattered with ewes and their recently born lambs, and dodged tractors and the occasional jogger brave, or perhaps foolish, enough to risk running along the unpavemented roads. Peter didn't talk much for the first part of the journey, focused as he was on navigating what to him were unfamiliar roads around my home, and for my part I was too busy worrying about exactly what I had gotten myself into to say much. However, once we made it off of the country lanes and onto more major A roads he started to open up a bit more, and by the time we reached the M25 and proceeded directly to a crawl he had become decidedly chatty indeed. I learnt a bit more about his son, who apparently worked for a tech firm doing something that Peter couldn't ever hope to explain, before he asked me if I followed the football and, without waiting for me to answer, started to pontificate at length about how his beloved West Ham stood a really good chance of beating Arsenal in their upcoming match, despite their abysmal and oh so typical showing against Man City last week, who, I was informed, they really should have thrashed with ease. After a while however the conversation turned to our plan of action, or more accurately our complete lack of one.

"So we drive to London and track down this Madam Josephine," I said, "and then what?"

"We talk to her," said Peter, as though it were the most obvious thing in the world.

"Ok," I said slowly. "And how exactly do you see

that going? Hello there Madam Josephine, sorry to bother you at your place of work but we were wondering if you happened to remember a fortune cookie you received around two years ago? Why, you ask? Well this honest to god police detective thinks that somehow supernatural forces from the other side are communicating with me secretly via automatic writing, that I am not aware of doing, and are passing on cryptic lifesaving messages to random people by way of those fortune cookies, and we were hoping you'd be able to tell us something of great importance that will aid us in our quixotic quest."

Peter gave me a sideways glance.

"Something like that," He said. "Though I'd suggest we dial back the snide git factor a few notches, if that's ok with you?"

I snorted slightly.

"And you think that will work?"

He shrugged.

"It worked on you," he pointed out. "Look, we go in, ask if she remembers anything and if she presses us for more details we say that we believe it will aid us with an ongoing investigation and leave it there."

"Right," I said, "and that works great until she reports me for impersonating a police officer and I go to jail."

"Woah," Peter said, lifting his hands momentarily off the steering wheel in a terrifying manner, "who said anything about impersonating a police officer? If it comes to a point where I feel I need to bring some authority to the proceedings I'll make sure she knows you are only a civilian consultant. Alright?"

I made a face.

"Well that very much seems like a distinction without a difference, and one that still ends with me sharing a very small room with a very large man named Chuck."

Peter laughed at this.

"I'm winding you up mate; we're just gonna go have a chat with her, nothing formal so nothing to worry about."

I lapsed into silence at this, feeling rather foolish, and slumped down in my seat a little. The traffic was moving better now and we would be heading into London proper in no time. Soon we would see what we would see, though I fully expected it to end with ridicule and laughter, because right now I was feeling that that was rather what we deserved. Peter shot me another glance.

"Don't be so glum," he said, "it'll be fine, you'll see, so chin up."

He went silent for a moment and his brow crinkled as if he were considering an important question that he wanted to ask me. I turned and looked at him expectantly and after a few moments he looked in my direction once more.

"So," he said seriously, "do you follow the

cricket?"

8

"A place of mystery may hold the very answers you seek."
The Wisdom of Zhu Zhuang, No. 722

As someone who lives ostensibly in the country London traffic was the stuff of nightmares and I was incredibly glad that I was not the one driving. For his part Peter didn't seem to be that bothered by the complete disregard London drivers seemed to have for the rules of the road, or for that matter the almost kamikaze like tendencies of the numerous cyclists shooting past at high speed in almost every conceivable direction, though the colour of his language did slant more to the blue end of the spectrum as we drove into the city.

I'd never been much of a fan of the city, and had only ever been to London a few times in my life. Too many people all trying to get somewhere in too much of a hurry for my liking. Laci's mum had written to me a while back, one of the many letters I never responded to and had now stopped opening altogether, and had mentioned that Laci's younger brother Darren was now living in the Big Smoke, though I couldn't for the life of me tell you where and had never even considered trying to visit, and yeah I know how that makes me look and you're probably not wrong. City life was very much not for me and I was already starting to feel well outside of my comfort zone just watching what seemed to be actual hordes of people passing by the window.

Peter, paying far less attention to the road than I was comfortable with, ran a search on the small laptop slash GPS slash Ed 209 looking device attached to his dashboard and was confident that we would indeed find Madam Josephine, aka Rachel Jones, at the occult bookshop mentioned in the Metro article, and so we set course for the Southwark borough of London. After that we drove around for what felt like the rest of the morning trying to find somewhere to park and when we finally did my surprise that it was still daylight was only partially sarcastic.

We found Aurora Books sandwiched between a hairdressers called the Divine London Looks Salon and one of those shops that sells nothing but the union flag plastered onto every object you could possibly conceive of. Clearly we were dealing with a quality establishment here. The outside of the shop was, of course, painted black, and the windows were jam packed with all manner of occult paraphernalia, from crystals to tarot cards, ankhs to wands, dreamcatchers to voodoo dolls. We pushed open the door and were greeted by the jingling of wind chimes and an almost overpowering smell of incense. I felt my head starting to swim immediately and I was tempted to suggest that I wait outside while Peter asked his questions but one look at his face told me he was as put off by the smell as I was and so I decided to soldier on.

While it was called a bookshop we had to weave our way through a great deal of other merchandise before we actually saw any books. The front half of the shop was given over to the sort of things that I thought would appeal more to wannabe weekend witches rather than anyone who would consider themselves the real thing. There were shelves holding a wide variety of decorative skulls and various sculptures of mythical beasts, heavy on the dragons and unicorns. Next to these was, as we had already ascertained, a large selection of incense and incense burners, and what looked to me to be a selection of Indian prayer rugs. There was an extensive collection of jewellery, masks and fake tattoos, as well as a whole section of the right hand wall which was given over to crystals of various sizes and another displaying nothing but Harry Potter merchandise, which struck me as a little too on the nose. Once we got past all that the shop seemed to open up a bit and we were treated to bookshelves running down the remaining length of the shop on either wall, at the far end of which sat a small counter, also, unsurprisingly, painted black.

Behind the counter sat a thin man in his mid-forties with silver hair and thick rimmed glasses, wearing an elaborately patterned yet finely tailored waistcoat over a black, short sleeved shirt. To complete the look he had on a western bolo tie, held together by what appeared to be a silver, runic version of Thor's hammer Mjölnir, something I recognised thanks to the Marvel films and not an education in Norse mythology. His overall appearance made me think of a failed lounge magician, or possibly the shopkeeper from Mr Benn, sans fez. When we approached the counter I expected Peter to draw his warrant card but the card, and his hands for that matter, remained firmly in his pockets.

"Excuse me," Peter said with a smile, "we'd like to speak to Madam Josephine if she's available?"

The thin man shifted his weight on the stool upon which he sat and looked us both over.

"Tarot readings are between 4 and 6 pm weekdays and are by appointment only. I'm afraid we are all booked up for this evening but if you would like I can see if I can slot you in at some time tomorrow."

Peter's smile never wavered.

"We're not here for a tarot reading," he said, his voice carrying the official tone he had used when first meeting me. "We would like to talk to her about something unrelated if that's possible?"

The thin man's eyes moved back and forth between us and it was clear that he was unsure what to make of us. I was pretty sure he had clocked Peter for a police officer from the moment he had walked through the door but as I was still sporting my retro farmer chic look I could tell he was having doubts. In the end he clearly decided that it was best to make this, whatever it was, someone else's problem and so, without taking his eyes from us, he twisted slightly and yelled back through the beaded door curtain that divided the shop from the back rooms.

"Madam Josephine, couple of gentlemen here to see you."

There was a pause before a tall woman in her late twenties, early thirties parted the beaded curtain and joined the thin man behind the counter. Her eyes snapped to us, glanced to the shopkeeper and then back to us before her mouth stretched in what appeared to be a completely genuine smile. She nodded her head in our direction and gave a small honest to god curtsey.

"I am Madam Josephine," she said, her voice soft,

her accent upper class, "how may I be of assistance officers?"

My eyebrows went up at this. Ok, it wasn't that impressive of a feat. Like I said Peter looked like the embodiment of every TV Detective Inspector you have ever seen in a post watershed crime drama, but the way she said it, the gravity that seemed to come with her words, well that made her very basic deduction that one, and therefore likely both of us were police officers seem like something more impressive, something much more in tune with why we had come to see her in the first place. Peter fixed her with his stone eyes for a second and I could tell he was trying to get a read on the woman. After a moment he seemed to come to a conclusion and decided to shift gears slightly.

"Rachel Jones?" he said in his official tone in a way that made it clear he wasn't here on shop business.

Madam Josephine cast her eyes between us and I got the same feeling of being read as I had received from Peter, and then, like a transition between two scenes in a movie, her demeanour changed perceptively and Rachel Jones spoke.

"That's me, how can I help you."

Her voice sounded stronger, more modern than moments before, and the posh accent had vanished completely, to be replaced by a slight northern twang. Now that was an impressive trick and even Peter seemed to skip a beat at the transformation.

"Umm, if we can have few moments of your time we'd like to talk to you about something, well something a little unusual, if that is ok with you."

Now it was Rachel's turn to express surprise.

"Huh," she said simply.

"So," Peter continued, "if we could maybe go somewhere private to talk that would be great."

"Wait," Rachel, said starting to rummage in a hidden pocket in the black lace, gothic style dress she was wearing, "I know why you're here."

Peter and I exchanged a look and when I turned back to Rachel she was smiling and I could tell at once that the smile she had offered us earlier had been far from genuine after all, because this one was the real deal.

"You're here because of this," she said with triumph.

She brought up her hand and between her thumb and forefinger she held a small off white rectangle, one centimetre by five and made from expensive vellum.

9

"The fates hold the answers, but their message is not always clear."
The Wisdom of Zhu Zhuang, No. 602

I reached out to grab the fortune but stopped my fingers a few inches short.
"Where did you get that?" I asked possibly a little too eagerly.
Rachel gave me a 'whoa there horsey' look and withdrew the fortune a bit.
"Where do you think? I got a takeaway last night," she explained. "The guy there told me he found it in a box yesterday afternoon when he was clearing out the storeroom. He was going to throw it out but he

thought it looked too nice for that so put on the shelf behind the counter, next to one of those waving cat things. Anyway when he saw me he decided to add it to my order as a little extra, I think he's a got a bit of a thing for me, though he did make me promise I wouldn't actually eat it as he couldn't say for sure how long it had been in that box."

She turned the fortune in her hand so that she could see the wording.

"I recognised it at once, only ever had one like it before, and it ended up saving a man's life. Of course, I didn't know that at the time and so threw that one away. Didn't make that mistake this time though."

I swallowed, my throat suddenly dry, though that could have been the incense.

"What does it say?" I asked.

Rachel smiled again. She held the fortune up, holding it at either end with forefingers and thumbs, and read.

"Look out for strangers seeking help tomorrow, for you hold the answer to their mystery."

I looked over at Peter who matched my look of surprise with one of his own. There was a part of my mind that still wanted to write this whole thing off as a coincidence, however it was currently being shouted down by the part of it screaming 'oh god, oh god magic is real'.

"That's you right?" Rachel asked. "You're the strangers and you have a mystery you think I can help solve?"

Peter nodded and held out his hand.

"May I?" he said, indicating the fortune.

There was a brief second of delay, something I had started to notice whenever one of my fortunes changed hands, before Rachel passed it over to him. He re-read the message and turned the fortune over in his hands a few times.

"It looks genuine," he said. "Just like the others, Zhu Zhuang, number two two one."

He looked at it for a few seconds more before passing it to me.

"What do you think?"

I didn't need as long as Peter to confirm it was the real thing, I knew my own work and had known we were dealing with a legitimate Steve Lander original the second Rachel had produced it. I checked it over anyway, dating it in my head from the material, as well as the colour and quality of the calligraphy.

"Yeah, definitely one of mine. A little newer than the one we opened this morning, but not by much, a few months maybe, six at the most."

"So," said Rachel, "that is why you're here, right?"

I nodded.

"Sort of. We came to ask you about the fortune you passed on to Daniel Phillips, we wanted to see whether you would be able to help us with our investigation," I passed the fortune back to her. "But I think that answers the question pretty conclusively, I'm not even sure if we need to know about the old fortune anymore."

Peter turned and gave me a look that clearly said 'oh, so you're running this investigation now are you' before looking back at Rachel.

"That said," he said with a smile, "if you wouldn't mind telling us about your encounter with Mr Phillips, we would appreciate it."

Rachel looked at the thin man who shrugged.

"Come with me," she said.

She lifted up a section of the counter and opened the front like a door so that we could pass behind it. We squeezed through and she closed the counter back up behind us.

"This way."

She led us through the beaded curtain, opened a door immediately to the left of it and led us up a narrow flight of stairs that turned sharply to the right, and then right again about halfway up. At the top we found ourselves in a short corridor with three doors leading off of it, one directly to the left of the stairs, one across from it and the last off to the right at the end of the corridor.

"This way," said Rachel again, opening the left-hand door for us.

I went first, Peter followed, and Rachel brought up the rear. Clearly at some point between the hallway and passing through the door I got myself lost, as rather than the upstairs room of a small bookshop in Southwark, London I found myself in a tent, or at least somewhere that bore a striking resemblance to one. Every wall of the room was covered in dark, flowing drapes embroidered with elaborate patterns in red, green and gold. The drapes were arranged so that they met in the centre of the ceiling from which hung, where one would usually find a modern light fitting, an old fashion brass lamp, though I suspected that the flame I could see flickering inside it was in fact an electric imitation. In the centre of the room was a circular table covered with a floor length cloth, again decorated with red, green and gold, and around it were positioned three high backed chairs, two on one side, one on the other, in the same colours. On the table sat three objects; two candles, real rather than electric ones this time, one in black the other in white, and a deck of large, ornate tarot cards.

Rachel moved one of the drapes and flicked a few switches hidden behind and the close, intimate, half-light of the room was replaced by the harsh glow of incandescent bulbs carefully hidden between the folds of the dark cloth. Rachel moved round to the single chair, gesturing for us to sit in the others.

"Sorry," she said as we sat, "it's not an ideal place to have a chat with the police, but it is the best we have I'm afraid, and we won't be bothered in here."

"It's fine," I said, giving her a smile. "And for the record I'm not with the police myself. Well I am with them, in the sense that I am here with him, but I am not *with* with them."

Rachel raised an eyebrow at this, and I decided it

would be best if I kept quiet for a bit. What's that saying? Better to be thought a fool than to open your mouth and prove it.

"So," said Peter acting as if I hadn't spoken, "what can you tell us about your encounter with Mr Phillips?"

Rachel sat up straight and smoothed down the front of her dress.

"Well I feel I should start by telling you that I am not actually psychic."

Neither Peter nor I responded to this.

"Well ok, you probably didn't think I was, but a lot of people do believe I have real powers and given that you are here to ask me about the fortune cookie thing I thought it was worth mentioning."

She reached out and started shuffling through the tarot cards in an absentminded fashion.

"When I first started working here there was another woman who used to do the tarot readings, Madam Katiana. She was something like twentieth generation pure Londoner, born and raised in Peckham, but you never would have guessed it as she could do the best Russian accent you've ever heard. She never broke character during working hours either; I'd been here almost two months before I found out. Anyway, she met this guy and ended up moving to Kent with him, much to the horror of her family. Well this left an opening in the shop and the tarot reader position was definitely a step up pay wise, so I volunteered."

She placed the shuffled deck back down on the table and cut it into three roughly equal piles.

"I studied psychology at university in Durham, and I knew from Madam Katiana that tarot reading was all about keeping things as general as possible and telling people what they wanted to hear. So, I borrowed one of the books from downstairs about the cards themselves and found a couple of videos on cold reading on YouTube. I practiced on my friends and family for a bit and once I could do it with a fair degree of competence Rob, that's the guy you met who owns the place, said I could try it out on actual customers, and well, I've been doing it ever since."

Rachel recombined the three decks, right on top of left, and then those cards on top of the central pile, before neatly aligning the cards and placing the deck directly in front of her.

"I'd only been doing it a few weeks when Daniel Phillips came to see me. I can't for the life of me recall what question he wanted answering, though I seriously doubt I told him anything more than vague generalities. I was still finding my feet you see back then and was, to put it bluntly, pretty crap. I had a tendency to fall back on the most basic interpretation of the cards, rather than offer anything approaching a more nuanced or personalised reading."

As she said this, she dealt out the top card of the deck and placed it in the centre of the round table.

"High Priestess, upright."

I noticed that her voice had slipped back into the soft, upper class accent she had used when we first met as she said this, though it seemed to me that this was an habitual rather than intentional act. I also got the impression that she was talking to herself rather than the two of us.

"Anyway," she continued, "when I got to the tenth card in the reading, that's the last one and the one that represents the likely outcome of the querent's current course of action, I completely blanked. I could not, for the life of me, remember what the card meant. What did pop into my head however was the fortune cookie I'd read the night before, and so I told him that."

She dealt out the next card, placing it diagonally across the first.

"The chariot, reversed."

There was a momentary pause and Rachel's brow crinkled ever so slightly, but whatever thought had entered her mind was quickly pushed away and she carried on with her story.

"Of course, I thought nothing more of it, just another reading, another twenty quid in my pocket. I would have probably forgotten it entirely if that reporter hadn't turned up a few weeks later."

She dealt the next card, placing it to the left of the others already on the table.

"The hermit, reversed," said Madam Josephine.

"He was a nice enough guy," said Rachel, "wanted

to know whether I knew that my prediction had saved someone's life or not. Pretty sure he made a joke about how I must already know, being psychic and all. Six of pentacles, upright."

The fourth card went on the right.

"Of course, I had no idea and when he started telling me the story I quickly realised that the apparently lifesaving prediction I'd made hadn't come from me at all, it had come from the fortune cookie."

A fifth card was dealt and placed above the two crossed cards.

"The star, upright."

There was a longer pause this time and Peter shifted in his chair.

"And, what happened next?" he asked.

"Hmm?" Rachel said, looking up. "Oh yes, well of course I was tempted to go with the lie, tell the reporter that I had seen the danger to his life clearly in the cards, maybe use the publicity to drum up a bit of business, you know."

She lay another card, this beneath the two central cards.

"Three of swords, upright. Oh, that is unfortunate."

She looked up from the cards.

"But I couldn't do it, it just felt, wrong, I don't know, but I decided to tell the truth instead. So, I explained that I'd read his fortune, not in the cards, but in a fortune cookie. Well the reporter, Ian, that was his name, Ian, oh what was it, Ian, Ian

Plummer, that was it. I remember because I thought at the time that it was amusing that he had an occupational surname that didn't fit with what he did for a living, you know? Well it made me smile anyway. Anyway, he loved the idea, started going on about that movie, the one with Leonardo DiCaprio and the spinney top thing, do you remember that movie?"

Another card was placed on the table, this time off to the right of the rest of the cards already laid out before us.

"Nine of wands, upright. Definitely some challenges ahead."

Now it was my turn to shift in my seat. My head was starting to spin with the speed at which Rachel flipped back and forth between personalities, her voice barely the same from one sentence to the next.

"All of that is in the newspaper article," I said, hoping to prompt her in the direction of new information, "is there anything else you can tell us about the event that wasn't reported?"

"Queen of swords, upright," she said, placing a card above the previous one. "And not really, I mean the article did bring in a few extra customers, but nothing to write home about. I tried to find the fortune but I'm pretty sure I threw it out with the empty takeaway containers, so it was long gone by that time. Kind of regret that really, would have been nice to still have it, what with all that happened."

Another card went down above the last one.

"Eight of cups, upright. Hmm now there's a common fear."

Rachel paused, her hand resting on the top of the deck.

"You know, now that I think about it there was something else," she gave her head a little shake. "No, sorry, it's silly, I doubt it would be of any help you at all."

"Please," said Peter, leaning forward slightly, "tell us, you never know what will help with an investigation, even the smallest details can be important."

Rachel shrugged.

"Well I don't see how this could be, it doesn't really have anything to do with Daniel Phillips, but alright. When I realised that I'd thrown out the fortune it kind of had a big effect on me. I got really rather upset about it, I mean disproportionately so. There were actual tears. I couldn't shake this feeling that I had, I don't know, lost something I guess, like I'd had my chance at something but now it was gone. It stuck with me for a while afterwards as well, which is silly as it was just a fortune cookie."

She sniffed, her eyes suddenly watering.

"Oh god, that embarrassing, I'm getting all emotional again thinking about it. You must think I'm a right idiot."

"Not at all," said Peter, passing her a tissue that seemed to have appeared out of nowhere.

"Thank you," Rachel said with a smile.

She lifted her hand off the top of the tarot deck to take the tissue and as she did so the top card slipped off of the deck and fell to the floor.

"Oh goodness," she said, her hand changing direction immediately to follow the card.

She picked it up and looked at it for a moment.

"Well that really is unfortunate," she said.

"What is it?" I asked.

She turned the card round and showed it to me. The card, like all the others she had dealt, was beautifully detailed. The card itself was black with a gold border and matching text. The image on the card was depicted in white outline and showed a tall tower, much as you might find attached to an old church, being struck by multiple bolts of golden lightning.

"The tower," Rachel said, "only I don't know which way up it should go."

"Does it matter?" I asked naively. "That's the final card right, the one that, what was it you said? The one that depicts the likely outcome of a person's actions if they stay on their current path, something like that."

She nodded.

"That's right, only if I place it upright it points to a future of chaos and upheaval, whereas if it was meant to be reversed," she turned the card upside down, "that suggests a chance of averting disaster and gaining some sort of transforming personal improvement. But I don't know which is right, so that's not good."

I looked at the card in her hand and then down at the ones spread across the table and suddenly it felt as though a great weight, physical, emotional, and maybe even metaphysical, had risen up from those nine pieces of cardboard to hang itself around my neck.

"No," I said, my eyes on the cards and a chill in my bones, "that's not good at all."

10

"What was lost will be found, and where you were alone you will find company."
The Wisdom of Zhu Zhuang, No. 89

I've never been a big believer in the supernatural. Ok, that's not exactly true. It would be more accurate to say that, up until fairly recently, I did not believe in the supernatural at all, and by fairly recently I mean within the last twelve hours or so. When we first met Laci had studied philosophy at university, before switching to a degree in social work in her second year, and when I'd started to develop an interest in her an interest in it had followed in due course. The two of us used to spend hours discussing the topic, whether we were walking hand in hand by the river deliberating on the nature of beauty, debating ethics over a grilled cheese sandwich, or arguing over whether it was possible to have objective knowledge whilst laying naked together in her dorm room bed, philosophy became a big part of our life together. On occasion things might have got a bit heated, but generally we would find ourselves in broad agreement, or at least be able to pin down exactly why we disagreed on a given issue.

One area where we really didn't see eye to eye, however, was on the nature of reality itself. Laci's metaphysics allowed for a world in which supernatural forces played a role, whereas mine very much did not. I was very much a philosophical naturalist, for me the natural was all that there was, there was no supernatural or spiritual component to the world, only the cold, logical laws and forces of nature. I did not believe in the soul, I would scoff at concepts like chi or vital energy, the idea that the moon could influence the number of people attending a hospital emergency room was ridiculous to me, and I most definitely did not believe in any kind of psychic power.

So as you can imagine as I sat there staring down at the laid out tarot cards and feeling, physically deep inside my body, the importance of the information contained in those cards, even though I had no idea what they meant, I was having something of a mild midlife metaphysical crisis. We had been guided here by a fortune cookie, a fortune cookie that I had created myself apparently under the influence of some otherworldly force, only to find that the person we wanted to talk to knew we were coming because they had read yet another of my fortunes the night before. Added to that it seemed to me that we were now being told that if we carried on with our investigation it would either end in chaos, fire and brimstone, or we would somehow stop said disaster from happening. So, no pressure then.

I looked over at Peter and could tell at once that he was not feeling the gravity of the moment as I was. He actually looked slightly disappointed and I could see his eyes moving back and forth as if he were trying to decide what we should do next.

"Right," he said, shifting his chair back a bit as if about to stand, "thank you very much, we appreciate your time."

Rachel looked at him in surprise.

"Is that it?"

Peter nodded.

"You've helped confirm a few things, thank you for that, but we don't want to waste any more of your time."

At this he stood and held out his hand for Rachel to shake. She eyed it for a moment and then reached up to take it. I cut in before their hands met.

"Wait, just wait a moment. She can still help; I know she can."

Peter looked down at me. He seemed to be considering what I had said but looked far from convinced.

"Think about it," I continued, "if she couldn't help why would the cookies have led us to her? Why would she have had a fortune of her own?"

He tilted his head slightly.

"It could just be a coincidence," he said, using my own words against me.

I shook my head.

"I, I don't think it is," I stammered.

"So, do you believe that something is really going on here? Something beyond the norm, something maybe even supernatural?"

I met his eye. I could feel the rational part of my mind throwing up excuses, telling me that there were any number of possible natural explanations for what was going on and that just because I couldn't think of them right that very moment it didn't mean they didn't exist. There was a term for what I was doing, something Laci had taught me all those years ago. It was called an argument from personal incredulity and I knew that logically it was completely invalid for me to conclude that something supernatural was at play here simply because I couldn't come up with an alternative. And yet that was what I believed, despite everything I had held to be true so far in my life I really, honestly did believe that something was at play here, something beyond anything that science, logic, or reason would recognise as real. I believed in the power of the fortune cookies. I believed that something or someone was sending messages through them to people in need. And I even believed in the accuracy of Rachel's tarot readings, even though she had told us herself that she was not psychic. After all, I had said the exact same thing to Peter and at the time I had been sure I was right too. I felt something shift in me as I acknowledged this to myself, and it felt both terrifying and freeing at the same time. My head swam with an almost physical tug at my memories and all at once I could practically see Laci standing there in the corner of the strange tent room, hands on her hips, lips slightly pouted, eyebrows raised, looking at me in that way she did when I finally realised she had been right about something all along, and I had just been too stubborn to accept it.

I nodded at Peter.

"Give her the bag," I said, my voice breaking ever so slightly.

Rachel looked at both of us in turn.

"What bag?" she asked.

In answer Peter reaching into one of his TARDIS like pockets and drew out the crumpled Tesco's bag. As he had done before in the café, he carefully emptied the contents on to the tarot card table, though of course now there were only seven of the original eight cookies remaining. Rachel looked at the fortune cookies and then back at us. I could tell from the expression on her face that she understood the depth of what was going on here.

"This is crazy," she said in a whisper.

"Pick one," said Peter, with a nod of his head as he sat back down.

Rachel leant forward and examined each of the small, wrapped cookies in turn. I had no idea what she was looking for but clearly she found it as, all at once, she reached out and plucked one of the cookies from the table. She held it in her hand for a moment, turning it this way and that, looking at it from every angle.

"This is the one," she said. "This is exactly like the one I had before, the one I lost, the one that saved David Phillip's life."

"Open it," I said, leaning forward myself now.

Rachel placed the cookie down on top of the remaining deck of tarot cards, then, with slightly awkward movements of her fingers, she untied the bow that held the top of the wax paper in place. She peeled the paper back like the petals of a flower and lifted the cookie free. She held it up before her face and let out a small laugh.

"Is it silly that I feel nervous?" she asked.

I shook my head.

"No, I felt the same way when I did it. It's odd, it feels…"

"Special," Rachel finished, "important."

I smiled.

"Yeah, exactly that."

She took a deep breath and, in one quick movement, cracked the cookie in half. She extracted the fortune, placing the cookie itself to one side, and, holding it in the same manner she had the first one, she read.

"There is no problem that can't be helped by a nice walk in the park."

Her face fell.

"I don't get it," she said.

"Can I see?" I asked.

With the usual slight hesitation, she handed me the fortune. I read the message again and noted the number, three hundred and seventy-two. I could well understand Rachel's confusion, she had likely been expecting something a bit more straight forward, but then she had not read Peter's book. I passed the fortune to him.

"Do you think it could be like the one Emma Billing got?" I asked.

He read the message himself and nodded.

"Yeah, I think you might be right."

"Umm, what do you mean?" said Rachel. "Who's this Emma Billing and what does she have to do with this?"

I briefly filled her in, leaving out the unsavoury details, and explained how, in the majority of cases we were aware of, the fortunes people received only seemed important after the fact and with full understanding of the situation.

"So, what now?" she asked.

I looked over at Peter.

"Now," he said, "we go to the park."

11

"Take the time to help others today, lift them up in their hour of need."
The Wisdom of Zhu Zhuang, No. 937

The three of us filed back downstairs, Rachel grabbing her coat from the room next to the one we had been sitting in along the way. Rob was still standing behind the counter and turned when we pushed our way through the bead curtain.

"Just popping out for a bit," Rachel said as she pulled on her coat.

Rob shrugged but otherwise didn't comment. Rachel's coat was a bulky puffer jacket with brown sleeves and three thick bands of colour, red, yellow, and green, running around the body. The style seemed completely at odds with the gothic look of the rest of her outfit and I got the feeling we were getting another glimpse of the real Rachel Jones rather than the Madam Josephine mask she wore during the working day. Rachel opened the counter for us to pass through again and we navigated our way out of the shop and onto the street beyond. I took a deep breath of the fresh, by London standards anyway, air; glad to be away from the cloying, sickly smell of the incense. The temperature seemed to have dropped a little while we had been in the shop and I pulled my coat closed and zipped it up. We huddled up close, forming a tight circle, and tried to make as small a blockage to other pedestrians as possible.

"So," said Rachel, "where exactly are we heading?"

Peter and I exchanged glances.

"We were kind of thinking you would know," I said.

"When you think of 'the park' what comes to mind," Peter said a bit more helpfully.

Rachel thought for a moment before turning and looking down the street.

"This way."

We walked for a few minutes before crossing over onto Borough High Street and then, a minute or so later, took a right down an alley way. We passed a playground on our left that sported a couple of swings, a few climbing frame slash slide contraptions, and a small roundabout, before turning left and stopping at a black wrought iron gate on our right. Rachel lifted the latch on the gate and pushed it open.

"Welcome to the park," Rachel said, holding up her hands.

The sign to the right of the gate told me that the area before me was called Little Dorrit Park, named after the Charles Dickens novel, and it was not at all what I had been expecting. When I think the word 'park' I think wide open spaces, a half dozen acres in size at least, but I guess I am a country boy after all. This was a city park and it was, small is not the right word for it, it was tiny. I was pretty sure I could have walked from one end of the park to the other in no more than ten seconds and half that for the width. A high fence that continued the wrought iron motif ran around three sides, with a taller, more modern, blue fence running down the left-hand side and cutting the park off from what appeared to be a school playground, though there were currently no kids in sight. A rough pathway of randomly spaced, broken paving stones stretched from the gate to the far end, a term I use very lightly, where a couple of tall, slender trees grew close to the fence. To our right and slightly depressed into the ground was a worn mosaic made of grey, white and terracotta stone that appeared to depict a bird and some flowers of some sort, and which was bordered all the way round by a couple of paving stone steps. Three blue metal benches, one on each of the three sides of the mosaic across from where we were standing, provided a place to relax and that, aside from a handful of bushes, a bin for rubbish and another for dog waste, was everything the park had to offer.

There was one other thing in the park however that immediately caught our attention. A man lay face down on the grass, head twisted slightly to one side, pretty much in the dead centre of the park. He wasn't moving.

Peter's training kicked in immediately.

"Call an ambulance," he barked, as he moved rapidly towards the prone figure.

Rachel followed him more slowly as I fumbled in my pocket for my mobile phone. Peter stopped a few feet away from the man and cast his gaze around the area. I have no idea what he was looking for but after a moment he seemed satisfied and dropped down to a knee beside the fallen man.

"Sir," he said speaking calmly but firmly, "my name is Peter, I'm a police officer, can you hear me?"

There was no answer. I hammered three nines into my phone and held it to my ear, my eyes locked on the scene unfolding before me.

"Sir, I'm going to touch your shoulder now," Peter continued.

He reached out and tapped two fingers against

the man's shoulder, not hard, but strong enough that you would definitely notice. There was still no response from the man.

"Emergency," sounded a voice in my ear making me jump, "which service do you require? Fire, Police or Ambulance?"

"Er, ambulance, we need an ambulance please."

There was a click, a pause, and a new voice came on the line.

"Ambulance services, can you please confirm the number you are calling from?"

This question took me by surprise but after a brief moment for my brain to catch up I dutifully rattled off my number.

"And can you tell me your exact location."

Again I paused for a second to think, even though I had only just seen the sign.

"I'm in Little Dorrit Park," I said a little too loudly, "off Borough High Street."

Before me Peter was checking the man over.

"Can you tell me what happened?" asked the operator in a voice that seemed unreasonably calm given the situation.

I opened my mouth then closed it again. My brain felt like it was running in slow motion and I was clearly not thinking straight. I had been about to tell her about our fortune cookie related adventures when I realised she probably didn't need to know that.

"We came to the park and we found a body, no,

sorry, not a body, at least I don't think it's a body, we found a man, he's on the ground, I'm not sure what happened to him."

Peter clearly heard my terrible attempt to relay the situation as he turned and yelled over at me.

"Steve, listen to me," he said in a measured tone. "Tell them that you have a single IC1 male, around 60 years of age who appears to have been attacked. Tell them he is breathing but unresponsive and that he has a head injury, though it is not currently bleeding. Tell them that there don't appear to be any other obvious signs of injury and that we are going to place him in the recovery position. And tell them there is a police officer on the scene."

The operator clearly heard most of what Peter had said, but I relayed everything he had told me again anyway.

"Can you confirm whether the attackers are still in the area?" the operator asked.

My eyes went wide at this and I swung round as though I expected to see a horde of masked hoodlums emerging from behind one of the small decorative bushes. But aside from the three of us and the injured man there was no one else in sight.

"No," I said, the relief obvious in my voice, "it's just us, no one else is here."

There was a pause.

"Ok sir, I am dispatching an ambulance to your location now. I will also be sending a police unit as well. Please stay on site until they arrive."

I thanked the operator and they told me that it was ok to hang up and it was only after I had done so that I realised I had absolutely no idea whether I had been talking to a man or a woman. I could remember nothing about the operator's voice other than their calm professionalism. I returned the phone to my pocket and, swallowing hard, I walked over to where the other two were crouched down beside the still unconscious man. I stopped a respectful distance away and when he realised I was there Peter stood up. He turned to face me and I saw that he was holding a wallet that I guessed belonged to the man, or the victim as I was starting to think of him, gripped at one corner with a folded over blue latex glove acting as a barrier between the leather and his fingers.

"Douglas Fairchild," he said. "Sixty-three, a local boy. There's still money in here and he's still got both his phone and watch, so it doesn't appear that this was a robbery."

I nodded. I wasn't really sure how I was meant to respond to this information. Sure, I watched plenty of crime drama on TV, but at the end of the day I was a country architect with a side line in preternatural baking, this was all a little out of my league.

"The ambulance is on its way," I told him.

He nodded and we both turned and looked back down at Mr Fairchild.

"Is he going to be alright?" I asked.

Peter shrugged.

"It's hard to tell. I suspect so, but he took a heck of a whack to the head, hard enough to make him lose consciousness, and that is never a good thing."

"Who do you think did it?"

Peter didn't answer straight away. Instead he turned in a small circle and looked around him.

"It's a fairly quiet area, but not enough that I would think it a likely location for a mugging. I mean anyone looking out of one of those windows over there," he pointed in the direction of the school, "or coming to visit the playground could have seen something. Plus, as I said, he still has all his valuables on him. No, I suspect that this was a spur of the moment thing. It's possible he got into an argument with a stranger, but I think it far more likely that it was someone he knew."

This took me aback a little. What Peter was saying made sense, but at the same time I couldn't imagine doing something like this to someone I knew, even the people I didn't like all that much. The sudden sound of sirens drifted to my ear and both of us turned to look back down the alleyway in the direction we had come from. One of the benefits of a big city like London was that you were never all that far away from an ambulance or police car if you needed one. The downside it seemed was that the chance of you actually needing one was probably higher than if you lived in a quiet little village like me.

"He's coming round," said Rachel suddenly.

We turned and saw at once that she was right. Mr Fairchild was moving and letting out a low moaning sound. He reached up to the wound on his head and winced when he touched it, his hand jumping back as though it had touched something hot.

"Easy there," said Peter, dropping down to one knee on the ground beside the man again, "try not to move, you've had a nasty bump on the head."

Fairchild looked at Peter, blinking hard as he did so.

"Who are...who are you?" he stammered.

"My name is Peter, I'm a police officer. These are my colleagues Miss Jones and Mr Lander. Can you tell me your name?"

I glanced at Peter in confusion as I knew he already knew the man's name having checked his wallet, which he still held between the folds of the latex glove, but then I realised what he was doing.

"My..my...I'm Douglas, Douglas Fairchild."

Peter smiled.

"That's good, very nice to meet you Mr Fairchild. Now, can you tell me what day it is?"

Fairchild thought for a moment and answered correctly.

"Good, that's very good. Ok, now the big question, do you know what happened to you?"

Again he seemed to think for a moment and then his eyes went wide.

"Oh god, Terry," he said, clearly alarmed.

"Terry?" repeated Peter. "Is that who did this to you?"

Fairchild looked at him in obvious confusion.

"What, no, of course not, Terry is just a boy, he's a good kid, he didn't," he paused as if uncertain, "he wouldn't do this, he wouldn't, not to me."

Peter nodded.

"Ok, so was Terry here with you when you were attacked?"

"No, no, of course not, Terry had nothing to do with this, he's a good kid, a good kid."

Peter reached out and placed a reassuring hand on Fairchild's shoulder.

"That's ok Mr Fairchild; try not to get yourself worked up now."

Fairchild clearly wasn't listening as he started moving as if trying to stand up.

"I've got to find him, I need to talk to him," he said, his voice rising in volume.

Peter applied a little more pressure to his hand on the man's shoulder in an attempt to keep him from moving.

"It's ok, you don't need to worry about him now, just look after yourself and you can tell him whatever you need to when you are back on your feet."

Fairchild slumped slightly and I could practically see the fight going out of him, but he wasn't entirely ready to give up yet.

"You don't understand, it's important, I need to talk to him now."

He made another effort to get up but all the exertion was clearly too much for him as suddenly, as if someone had cut his strings, he collapsed back, his eyes rolling up and his head lolling to one side. Peter managed to grab him and stop him from hitting the ground hard. He lowered him back down and checked that he was still breathing. At that moment there was the sound of the gate opening behind us and a voice barked out in command.

"Make room please, coming through."

We all turned to see two paramedics, one man and one woman, coming through the gate and hurrying towards us. We all backed off immediately and let them get to work. Given the size of the park there weren't many options as to where to stand and we found ourselves stepping down to stand on the mosaic. We stood in silence for a few moments watching the paramedics and then Rachel turned to face us.

"Is this what you thought would happen?" she asked.

"What?" I said. "What do you mean?"

"Well you clearly expected to find something, otherwise why did we come here? So did you expect to find something like this?"

"No," I said.

"Yes," said Peter, "well not this exactly, but

something along these lines certainly."

I turned to face him.

"You did?"

He shrugged.

"Sure, look, like it or not but almost every situation that I've come across where one of your fortunes has been involved has had something to do with someone or other in a life or death situation. With very few exceptions that has always been the pattern. So yes, when Miss Jones here picked that fortune and led us to this park I did think there was a chance that we could encounter something like this."

Rachel and I both looked at him for a moment. Again it was Rachel who broke the silence.

"So, do you think we were meant to stop this?" she asked. "That if maybe I hadn't spent so long telling you my life story we might have got here in time to stop it happening?"

I could tell by the slight crack in her voice that she could feel the weight of responsibility settling on her shoulders, and she wasn't the only one. My mind was running through all the things we had done so far that day, trying to work out if there were things we could have done differently that would have led us here sooner, in time to stop Mr Fairchild from being attacked. Peter shook his head.

"No, no, I don't think that is the case, and you shouldn't either."

He took a deep breath.

"Look, I've been investigating these fortunes for two years now and in every case that I've come across I have never found even a single instance where bad things have happened because people didn't act fast enough. Without exception people have either done what the fortune said or not, it's always been a binary thing. We did what it said and I truly believe that we got here when we were meant to, and that for some reason we were not meant to stop this from happening. Now that does not mean I don't feel like shit for not being here to stop it, because I do, but I believe, I have to believe, that we are here now," he emphasised the word "because we are meant to be here now."

I looked over at Rachel and she met my eye. It was clear she was still not happy about the situation, but at the same time she seemed a little more resolute than she had a moment before.

"Ok," she said, "so if we weren't meant to stop him from being attacked what are we meant to do?"

I looked back at Peter and he gave me a half smile and I could tell he was thinking the same thing I was.

"I think," I said, "that we need to find Terry."

12

"When you seek you may find you already know where to look."
The Wisdom of Zhu Zhuang, No. 1003

The paramedics were starting to load Mr Fairchild onto a stretcher when a couple of uniformed police officers showed up. Peter went over to talk to them, flashing his warrant card as he did so. One of them pulled out a notebook and started scribbling down whatever Peter was saying.

"So," said Rachel beside me, "does this sort of thing happen to you often?"

I almost laughed.

"God no, this is a first. Until he turned up at my

house last night," I said gesturing at Peter, "I had a nice normal life, pretty boring actually. This is all as new to me as it is to you."

"But, I'm right in thinking that you made the cookies? That it's your fortunes that are doing all this."

I looked at her and could tell she wasn't exactly sure what to make of me. I nodded.

"Yeah, I made them, but I promise you I have absolutely no idea what is going on here. I had no idea that any of this was happening until last night. Heck, you've known about them helping people longer than I have. It was just a hobby, one that I turned out to be good at and that made me a bit of money on the side. I never intended to try and help people like this, and I sure as hell didn't know I was predicting the future."

Rachel eyed me for a moment and then seemed to come to a decision.

"Ok," she said, "I believe you. You look even more shaken up by all this than I feel. If you knew it was going to happen I expect you'd be a lot less affected."

I smiled.

"Or maybe I'm a super villain," I said, thinking back to Peter's comment from that morning.

Rachel's eyebrows went up at this.

"Sure, yeah, that," she said.

Suddenly feeling foolish I looked back towards Peter in time to see him handing over the wallet to one of the police officers who dropped it into a clear plastic bag. A sudden idea occurred to me and before I had time to think it through I found myself walking towards them. As I did so I reached into the pocket of my coat and pulled out the old Tesco bag that held the remaining six cookies. When we were getting ready to leave the book shop I had collected up all of the cookies from the table and dropped them back into the bag and, for reasons I still wasn't sure of, rather than returning it to Peter I had stuffed it into my own pocket. Now, as I approached the three police officers, I stuck my hand into the bag, drew out a cookie completely at random before sticking the bag back into my pocket.

"Here," I said as I reached them, "he dropped this as well."

I held up the cookie and Peter shot me a look as if to ask if I was sure about what I was doing. I nodded and he shrugged.

"Thank you," said the younger of the two uniformed officers. "We will be sure he gets it."

He held out the bag and with only a slight hesitation I dropped it inside. The officer smiled, folded up the bag and the two of them moved off to follow the paramedics who were now carrying Fairchild back toward the ambulance.

And then there were five.

Rachel came over to join us.

"What was that about?" she asked.

I opened my mouth, and then closed it again. I

really wasn't sure why I had given Fairchild one of the cookies, I'd just had the feeling that he should have one, that it was important that he had one.

"It felt right," I said lamely.

Rachel looked at me for a second before nodding.

"Ok, that's enough for me. So now what?"

We both looked to Peter, as he always seemed to know what our next step should be. He didn't disappoint.

"I think we should go back to my car," He said.

With a last quick look around the three of us left the park and walked back down the alley-way to Borough High Street. The paramedics had finished loading Fairchild into the back of the ambulance and I caught a glimpse of him as they closed the door. I was encouraged to see that he appeared to have regained consciousness once more though he still appeared to be as agitated as he had been earlier and was resisting the paramedics attempt to put a mask over his face to help with his breathing.

"Where are they taking him?" I asked as we drew level with the older of the two police officers.

The officer eyed me for a moment, clearly debating if he should tell me, someone who was not related to Mr Fairchild and could, for all he knew, have been involved in his assault, anything about where the injured man was going. But, after a glance at Peter, he clearly concluded that if I was chumming around with a detective I probably wasn't a hardened criminal and so decided to answer.

"They'll take him to Kings; they'll take good care of him there."

I thanked him for the information and then Peter and he shared a few more words, the former promising that we would be available for interviews if needed and passing over one of his business cards. After that, as the ambulance pulled out into traffic, the three of us left the police officers and headed back down the street in the direction we had come from.

When we reached the car Peter quickly unlocked it and jumped in.

"Would you like to call shotgun?" I asked Rachel.

Rachel looked at me, then at the car, then off down the road in the direction of the shop. I could tell that she was concern by how long she had been away already.

"I'm sure Rob will understand," I said, opening the door for her, "I mean it's not every day that you find an unconscious man in the park. Well, at least it's not for me; I'm not sure what it's like in the city. You could be tripping over unconscious people all the time for all I know."

Rachel smiled.

"Only on the weekends," she said, as she climbed into the passenger seat, "but for most of those it's self-inflicted."

I opened the rear passenger door and climbed in behind her. Peter already had the Ed 209 fired up and was running a search on Douglas Fairchild. He turned it so that we could all see the screen.

"Ok, here he is, Douglas John Fairchild, no criminal record, though it does look like he was the victim of a burglary a few years back, poor bugger."

Peter tapped a few more keys bringing up a new page on the screen.

"Got divorced about fifteen years ago now, no sign that he ever remarried, though," he clicked a couple of links, "it does appear that there is an Irene Thompson who shares the same address so it looks like he might be giving living in sin a try."

Peter fell silent for a moment as he navigated between what appeared to be several different databases.

"Ok, this is what I was looking for, next of kin. Right, seems that he has a daughter, one Mary Jackson, married with, ah yes, two children, who are…" more tapping, "both girls, neither of whom are called Terry or really even anything close."

I felt my shoulders slump. I'd been convinced he was onto something there and was rather caught up in the whole thing, I felt like I was in an episode of CSI or something, even though Peter was the one doing all the actual leg work. Peter took a deep breath and looked out of the window for a moment.

"Ok, new idea," he said, turning back to the computer.

He flipped back through a few of his previous searches until he found Fairchild's address details again.

"Let's take a look at Irene instead shall we."

As he had done before he quickly brought up some information on Ms Thompson in a manner that suddenly struck me as both a little intrusive and alarming. When he had been looking into Fairchild directly it had seemed like a natural next step in our bizarre investigation, but looking at the woman he lived with struck me as a little off course. Which is probably why I am not a detective as, in less than thirty seconds, Peter had our man, or more precisely our boy.

"Terry Taylor, aged thirteen, grandson to Irene Thompson. Hmm, seems he's got a bit of record, Mr Fairchild might have spoken a bit too soon when he said he was a good kid. Let's have a look."

He clicked a link and Terry's record popped up on the screen and we all got our first look at the kid. The processing photo showed a skinny looking, mixed race boy with a mess of curly hair and a spattering of acne around his chin who was managing the impressive feat of looking both absolutely terrified and defiant at the same time. He was clearly trying to act tough but there was a redness to his eyes that spoke of someone moments from tears.

"Ok, so it seems he was picked up a couple of times for vandalism, nothing major, just a bit of graffiti, seems he considers himself an artist. By the looks of things the police were happy to let him off with a warning; it was actually his father who insisted that he be fully processed through into the system. Clearly a fan of the scared straight approach, though I guess it must have worked as that appears to be the last time he was on our radar. That or he's got better at running away."

I thought for a moment about the area around the park.

"There was a school next to the park," I said. "Do you think Fairchild went there to try and see Terry?"

Peter shook his head.

"I doubt it. There are actually two schools next to the park, St Josephs and the Cathedral School, but they're both primary schools so Terry would be too old for either. Plus, judging from the address on his file I doubt it he would have attended either of those schools anyway, too far away. Whatever Mr Fairchild was in that park for I'd be willing to bet it wasn't anything to do with the schools."

We all lapsed into silence for a moment as we all considered what a man in his sixties would be doing hanging out in a park sandwiched between two primary schools in the middle of the day. I'm sure I wasn't the only one whose mind went somewhere dark.

"So now what?" asked Rachel. "How do we go about finding this kid, if that's even what we are planning to do?"

"Could we put out an APB or something?" I

suggested.

Peter turned in his seat and gave me a look.

"You've been watching too much TV," He sighed. "Mr Fairchild said that Terry wasn't in the park with him, assuming that he was telling the truth, and assuming that he had already looked in the obvious places, like his school, his house, that sort of thing, then to be honest I'm not sure I know where to start. It's a bit of a mystery."

Rachel sat forward at this.

"What did you say?"

Peter raised a bushy eyebrow.

"I said I have no idea where to start."

"No, not that bit," said Rachel, unzipping her coat and fumbling in her dress pocket, "the bit about it being a mystery."

She pulled out the fortune again; the one she had shown us when we first met her at the book shop.

"I thought this was an instruction that I should help you in general, but now I am thinking it might be a bit more specific than that."

She passed the fortune to Peter who looked at it and read it out loud again.

"Look out for strangers seeking help tomorrow, for you hold the answer to their mystery. The Wisdom of Zhu Zhuang, number two two one."

"Maybe you two aren't the only strangers I am meant to help, maybe I'm meant to help Mr Fairchild as well, maybe that's the mystery I hold the answer to, finding Terry."

Peter and I just looked at her for a moment.

"Ok," I said, "I'm happy to go with that. So, do you know where he might be?"

Rachel smiled.

"I think I do."

13

"Listen to the young, for they may hold answers to questions you have never thought to ask."
The Wisdom of Zhu Zhuang, No. 772

Leaving the car where it was, Rachel led us first north and then in a roughly south-easterly direction across the city. We walked down St Thomas Street, passing the towering magnificence of the Shard skyscraper along the way. I craned my head back looking up at it as we passed by on the opposite side of the street. Even in the low light of the cold day the ninety-five-storey building of glass and steel shone as it stabbed its way into the grey sky. I felt a little dizzy looking up at it, it was so damn tall, so quickly returned my gaze to where we were going. We continued on, passing the sprawling brick clad side of London Bridge Station which seemed to me as long, if not longer, than the Shard was tall. As we walked down the road I could see the brickwork of the station visibly aging, as though with every step we were travelling further back into the past. By the time we had crossed over a five-way junction and onto Crucifix Lane the modern station was long behind us and we were firmly back in the Victorian era. The bricks were darker, stained by years of weather and passing vehicles, and the various archways and facings were in an obvious state of disrepair. We passed through an old tunnel beneath the railway lines and as we emerged on the other side we found ourselves walking beside a fence made of what appeared to be old scaffolding poles.

"Here we are," said Rachel, gesturing at the fence with her hand without actually removing it from the pocket of her puffer jacket.

Looking along the fence I could make out the words 'White Grounds' written across the scaffolding poles in large yellow letters and from beyond the fence I could hear bangs, and clacks, and yells, and a constant rumble that sounded to me not unlike some sort of tiny train passing by on the tracks above.

"Where is here exactly?" I asked.

"This," Rachel said as she led us around the corner and through a gate in the fence, "is White

Grounds Skatepark, and based on how things have been going today I think this is where we will find Terry."

We stopped just inside the gate and looked around, taking the place in. The skatepark it seemed was based inside another of the tunnels running beneath the railway lines that had been given over to the youth of the city for their enjoyment. Florescent tubes, placed where the ceiling started to curve over, cast what would have otherwise been a dark and rather gloomy tunnel into bright relief. The floor was smooth concrete and along each side of the tunnel there were various ramps, and steps, and slopes along, over, and off of which people could skateboard, and in fact around a half dozen teenagers, mostly boys, were currently doing just that. But more importantly from our point of view was the fact that every single vertical surface in sight was completely covered with graffiti.

"The state park is a legal graffiti zone," Rachel explained. "You said that Terry's file showed that he had been in trouble for graffiti in the past but that there was nothing recent. You suggested that meant he had either stopped or got better at running from the police. Well that got me wondering if maybe he picked option C instead."

Peter gave an impressed grunt at this and the three of us started heading down the tunnel looking for the boy we had seen in the processing photo. As we did the teenagers we passed stopped zipping about on their skateboards and watched us. There was no open hostility but I got the distinct impression that we were not wanted here and I heard more than one whispered derogatory term aimed in our direction and in reference to Peter's chosen profession. Peter clearly heard them too as he hunched his shoulders and his face grew stern, but other than that he chose to ignore them, which I thought was probably for the best. We neared another gate at the far end of the tunnel only to find that the skatepark branched off to the right and continued down a side tunnel that connected it to the one we had walked down earlier, though a fence that reached most of the way to the ceiling made access impossible at that end. There were a couple of high, jump-like ramps down this tunnel, and squatting beside the first of them, spray can in hand, was the very person we were looking for.

"Terry Taylor," Peter called out in a voice that even I found intimidating.

I winced as Terry looked up and took us all in. Three adults he didn't know were walking towards him, one of them a large, angry looking man who was clearly a police officer. It didn't take a rocket scientist to work out what a kid with a history of getting into trouble with the police would do in a situation like this. He ran. Unfortunately for him he decided to head further down the side tunnel rather than trying to get past us and there was simply no way out in that direction. Which didn't stop him from trying. He scrambled up the ramp at the end of the tunnel and threw himself at the fence. He got a firm enough grip on it that he didn't immediately fall back down, but he didn't appear to be going anywhere fast.

"Oi, cut that out," Peter yelled, as he jogged over to stand at the bottom of the ramp. "You're not in trouble; we just want to have a word. Douglas Fairbanks sent us."

At the sound of Fairbanks' name Terry stopped trying to scale the fence and turned, still hanging from it, to look down at Peter.

"Gramps sent you?" he asked, clearly unsure.

Peter paused for the briefest of seconds and then nodded. In those few short words Terry had told us a lot more about his relationship with Fairchild.

"Yes, so come down."

He took a breath and continued in a softer tone.

"Look Terry, we just want to have a quick word, you're not in trouble, you've done nothing wrong, so you have nothing to worry about."

Terry kept looking at Peter for a few seconds before raising his gaze and looked past us. I turned to see that the teenagers had gathered in a group and were standing a few feet back from the mouth of the side tunnel. I could tell that Terry was weighing up the effect that being seen talking to the police would have on his street cred.

"You said this is about my granddad, right?" he said, in a voice loud enough to carry to the group of teens.

"Yes, that's right, so come down now will you."

Terry glanced at the teens once more then clearly made his decision as he dropped effortlessly back down to the top of the ramp.

"Alright," he said, his voice cocky, "but you'll have to buy me lunch first."

This raised a laugh from the teens and Terry smiled, clearly happy that he had done enough to placate his peers in this matter. He slid back down the ramp as Rachel and I walked over to stand next to Peter. Up close and at ground level Terry seemed strangely smaller than he had from a distance. He still had a certain swagger to him but from this distance I could see that a lot of it was clearly an act and it was apparent that despite his best efforts he was still just a boy. I felt bad about what we were about to tell him.

"Terry," Peter said, "I'm sorry to have to tell you this, but we've got some bad news about your grandfather."

I saw fear flood over the kid's face and though he did his best to control it his top lip quivered slightly.

"What's happened, is he alright?"

"He's in good hands; he's been taken to King's College Hospital. It appears as though he was attacked."

Terry put his hands to his face.

"Oh god, oh shit, sorry, oh man, you have to take me to see him."

I almost smiled at his instant apology for swearing and got the feeling that a kid whose father would make sure the police processed him into the system for a bit of graffiti probably had something to say about his son swearing as well. Peter continued.

"We will Terry, we will, but you need to answer some questions first. Do you have any idea who might have done this to your grandfather?"

Terry looked at Peter in horror, but I could tell he was giving the question some serious thought. After a few moments he shook his head.

"No, no one, Gramps was a great guy, always looking out for everyone ya know. He was the best thing to happen to Nan, her old husband was a dick, sorry, but he was."

"Ok, that's ok. When we spoke to him though he said he was looking for you and he seemed really worried, as though you were in some sort of trouble. Do you have any idea what that could have been about?"

It's an old cliché that gets used a lot when describing someone getting a shock. I'd never actually seen it in person before, but it really did look like the blood drained out of his face at Peter's words. He even staggered a bit, all of which made the fact that he denied knowing what we were talking about a little comical.

"No, no idea, I've not done anything."

Peter cocked his head slightly to one side.

"No one said that you did anything, just that your grandfather was worried about you. Why would you think that meant you did something?"

My eyes flicked between him and Terry. I could see the boy closing up, he was worried about his grandfather sure, but he was more worried about getting in trouble with the police again. I decided to play a hunch, though admittedly one with a pretty good track record so far. I reached into my pocket, rummaged round a bit and pulled out one of the fortune cookies. I held it up so that Terry could see it clearly.

"Do you know what this is?" I asked.

Terry turned and looked at the cookie and a puzzled expression crossed his face.

"Yeah, it's a fortune cookie. Where'd you get it? My Nan had one just like it."

The three of us exchanged looks.

"Really?" I said. "Can you tell us about it."

He looked at me as if I was crazy for a moment then shrugged.

"Not much to tell, my Nan had one; I found it on a shelf behind some old photos the other night. I asked if I could have it, she said yes."

All three of us stared at him for a few seconds.

"And?" I said finally.

"And what? I ate it; it tasted alright, a little stale."

"And what did the fortune say?"

Terry looked at each of us in turn clearly a little unnerved by how intense we were all suddenly looking. He reached into his pocket and pulled out a blue wallet with the Captain America shield logo on the side. He opened it, delved into one of the card slots and pulled out an all too familiar piece of vellum. He looked at it, looked at me, hesitated as I knew he would, and handed it over. I flipped it round and, as had become the norm for me now, read it out loud.

"A secret shared is a burden halved. The Wisdom of Zhu Zhuang, number 1023."

Peter gave me a look.

"A little derivative don't you think?"

I shrugged.

"They can't all be originals," I said. "Plus, it's a classic."

Rachel frowned at us.

"Cut it out you two, you're missing the point," she turned to face the kid. "Terry, you had a secret didn't you, and after you read the fortune you told your grandfather. I'm right, aren't I?"

Terry's mouth fell open and he nodded his head.

"How did you know that?" he asked in amazement.

Rachel smiled and gave him a quick wink.

"I have my ways," she replied. "But what's important is that you did share your secret with your grandfather, and I think something about it got him worried enough about you that he came looking for you this morning. He came looking for you and for some reason he thought you might be in

Little Dorrit Park. That's where we found him, that's where he was attacked."

Terry's eyes grew wet but his jaw set hard and it was suddenly as though I was looking at his processing photo again. Conflicting emotions were boiling up inside him. Anger, fear, sorrow, all showed on his face, mixed together with teenage defiance and the rebellious spirit of a kid who came to a skatepark to paint.

"Aww man, I told him not to get involved," he said, his voice cracking, "I told him I could handle it myself. Why didn't he listen?"

Rachel smiled again, only this time it was full of comfort and concern.

"Terry, we can help you, but you need to let us. You need to tell us what you told your grandfather."

Terry looked at each of us in turn again. I could practically see his mind working as he weighed up his need to do right by his grandfather, his urge to keep his secret, and his concern that the last time he told someone they got hurt.

But after a moment more, he came to a decision.

14

"Old faces and new all have their part to play."
The Wisdom of Zhu Zhuang, No. 92

The four of us headed back to Peter's car, three adults on a magical mystery tour, and one rather confused and upset teenager whose day we had pretty much ruined. We all bundled into the battered Ford Focus, Peter in the driving seat of course, Rachel beside him once more, and Terry and I stuck in the back. Peter took all our lives in his hands as he pulled out into London traffic and after another terrifying, though mercifully short, drive we arrived at King's College Hospital. We followed the narrow one-way system that ran around the hospital until we reached the visitors carpark, and after completing a few laps of it managed to squeeze into a space as someone pulled out to leave. We walked back the way we had come and out onto the main road to find the entrance to the emergency department.

Once inside we again let Peter's badge do the talking. Approaching the reception area with a flash of his warrant card he asked about Douglas Fairchild, explaining that Terry was a relative. The nurse behind the counter tapped a few keys on her computer and informed us that he was stable but in recovery and that we were welcome to go down to the waiting area, although we couldn't see him at present. Peter thanked her and the four of us headed off in the direction she indicated. It had been several years since I had been in a hospital and I was finding that the whole experience was bringing back some upsetting memories. I could remember walking corridors like these back when it had been Laci lying in a hospital bed after her operation. We were in a different part of the country but so many things were the same. The silver grey colour of the floors, the local art and half empty information racks that covered the walls, the disinfectant smell that spoke of cleanliness, but which only reminded me of death. Even the doctors looked the same to me I thought as we passed a tall, efficient looking, dark haired man in blue hospital scrubs.

"Mr Lander?"

I turned to find myself looking at an expression of pleasant surprise written across the familiar face of a man I knew well, liked even, and yet had hoped I'd never see again. I swallowed.

"Dr Hanson," I said, "what are you doing here?"

Dr Mackenzie Hanson smiled at me and stretched out a hand for me to shake, almost crushing my fingers in the process.

"I should be asking you the same thing," he said with a hint of laughter in his voice. "I work here, been here a few years now."

I nodded, unsure what to say. Eventually I found my voice.

"I'm here to see a friend," I lied.

I didn't want to take the time to explain what was actually going on to Dr Hanson; I didn't want to talk to him at all for that matter. Don't get me wrong, he's not a bad guy. He was always so kind and generous and understanding and diligent, everything you would want in a doctor. It's just that the last time I'd seen him he'd said something that made me kind of hate him. Three little words that carried all the weight of the world. Time. Of. Death. That's the kind of thing that you don't forgive. I'm sure all of my conflicting emotions were playing across my face as Dr Hanson frowned slightly and his voice became soft, concerned.

"Everything alright Steve, you hanging in there?"

I swallowed again; worried I might gag on whatever the hell kept rising up in my throat.

"Yeah," I croaked, "yeah, I'm good, doing well thanks."

It was obvious I was lying, but Hanson was too nice a guy to call me on it, the bastard.

"Well good, I'm glad to hear that," he said with a warm smile. "You're a good guy, you deserve to be happy."

Part of me wanted to hug him at this, throw my arms around him and weep in the presence of one of the few people who actually knew the things I had been through. Another part of me wanted to hit him and never stop. I thought it best to keep still as I wasn't at all certain which of the two physical reactions would win out.

"Well," said Hanson, "it was good to see you Steve, and I'm glad to see you out with friends, even if you are visiting a hospital."

I mumbled something in response and managed a smile. Hanson nodded to the others before turning and walked off in a manner that somehow managed to convey both that he didn't have a care in the world and that he had to be somewhere very important indeed. I watched him go and as he rounded the corner and disappeared from sight I realised two things. The first was that my eyes were moist and threatening tears. The second was that I was clenching my fists so tight that my fingernails were digging into my skin. I took a deep breath and in one movement released my fists and whipped my eyes. I turned to face the other. None of them said anything.

"Right," I said, but the word came out as a whisper so I tried again. "Right, shall we get on then?"

Peter nodded, Rachel gave me a kind smile that actually did make me feel a bit better, and Terry rolled his eyes and mouthed something that was probably insulting under his breath. We continued down the corridor and soon found the waiting room. We pushed through the double doors and had barely made it a step inside when a tall, older, though none the less striking for it, black woman rose from her chair and walked rapidly towards us arms held out. I was a little taken aback for a moment until Terry pushed past me and hurried towards her.

"Nan," he cried, running into the woman's arms with the enthusiasm of a much younger boy.

Irene Thompson enclosed her grandson in a crushing embrace, her strong face a mix of conflicting yet well controlled emotions. After a moment she released Terry and shifted him bodily to stand at her side before fixing the three of us with a questioning and authoritative gaze. She reminded me a lot of Angela Bassett, though she was a good few years older than the actress, as they both possessed the same formidable presence, something about the eyes I think.

"And who might you be?" she asked in a voice that was prime London with just a hint of Caribbean at the edges.

"I'm DI Peter Fuller; these are my associates Mr Lander and Miss Jones."

Irene shot her grandson a look that I am sure would have withered flowers.

"What trouble have you got yourself into this time boy?" she demanded.

"No Nan, it's not like that," Terry pleaded, "they came to get me because of Gramps. I promise, I ain't in any trouble, swear."

"He's telling the truth Mrs Thompson, he's not in any trouble at all."

Irene turned her eyes on us again and for a moment the withering effect remained, but it lifted in an instant and she gave a smile that was equal parts pride, warmth, and complete and total love and affection.

"Well that is good to hear. He's a good boy really, just a bit silly in the head at times," she said, reaching out and gently smacking the back of Terry's head who winced then smiled.

For a moment I found myself in the unusual position of both wishing she were my grandmother and being glad that she was not. I was pretty sure I knew where Terry's Dad got his strict approach to discipline from. Peter took a step forward.

"Mrs Thompson, do you mind if we ask after the condition of Mr Fairchild?" he asked.

Irene lifted her chin as if challenging our right to ask such questions but ultimately deigned to answer.

"He is asleep right now. He took a nasty hit to the head, but that nice Dr Hanson said he should make a full recovery."

"Oh," I said at the mention of Hanson, "he does."

Irene turned her full attention on me at this and I am not too big to admit I felt rather uncomfortable under her gaze.

"What is that meant to mean?" she demanded. "Do you know something I do not?"

I shook my head.

"No, I'm sure it's all fine, he, well he was my wife's neurologist, that's all."

Irene's eyes narrowed as she scrutinised me for a moment in a manner that gave stony eyed Peter a run for his money. This woman would have made a great cop. I wasn't lying, my reaction had indeed simply been a response to knowing that the same doctor that had treated Laci in her final days was also looking after Douglas Fairchild, and yet at the same time I did feel that there was something disturbing about this fact, though I could not have put my finger on it for the life of me. I am not sure what she saw in me, but her gaze softened a little and while she did not seem fully satisfied with my response, she seemed willing to let it lie for now. Thankfully Peter cut in again, drawing her attention back to him.

"We were hoping that we would be able to have a quick word with Mr Fairchild if that is possible?

We would like to ask him about the attack and about another issue that has come to our attention."

"I'm sorry but that is not possible, as I said he is asleep right now and he needs his rest."

Peter nodded.

"Of course, Mrs Thompson, we completely understand."

He reached into his pocket and once again pulled out a business card and a biro. He quickly scribbled on the back of the card and handed it over to Irene.

"This is my mobile number; I would greatly appreciate it if you would give me a call when he is feeling well enough to talk."

Irene examined the card with a look of mild distaste but nodded.

"I will do that detective, thank you for your understanding."

There was an awkward silence and before Peter returned the nod and led Rachel and me back out into the corridor. As soon as the door closed, I turned to face him.

"So now what?" I asked.

"Yeah," said Rachel, "I mean nice as it was to meet Terry's Nan it all feels a little anticlimactic. I was expecting to get some sort of answer to, well, something, anything."

Peter shrugged.

"Agreed, but I am sure we will get answers later. As for now," he looked at his watch, "I think it's time we got something to eat."

15

"If you don't feed the body then how can you expect to feed the mind?"
The Wisdom of Zhu Zhuang, No. 437

We sat at a small table in the hospital canteen eating greasy burgers, overly salted fries, and drinking half a litre each of sugar heavy fizzy pop. And no, the irony was not lost on me. We didn't talk much, not that there wasn't a lot to discuss; it was just that none of us really knew where to start. So instead we ate in silence, lost in our own thoughts about the events of the day. It seemed somewhat crazy to me that only yesterday I had been a hardened sceptic, dismissing Peter's wild ideas about psychic fortune cookies as the ravings of a mad man. And yet now here I was, fully invested in the idea and traipsing all over London in a wild attempt to work out what the hell it could all mean. Screwing up the burger wrapper and wiping my mouth with a napkin I decided to break the silence.

"Ok, so just to recap and to bring Rachel fully up to speed, let's run through how we got where we are."

Peter swallowed a mouthful of chips.

"Last night I came to talk to you about the fortune cookies you make and how they keep turning up at crimes scenes," he said. "I was pretty sure that you had to be some kind of psychic."

"But I'm not," I cut in.

"At least not a conventional one."

"Fine, at least not a conventional one," I agreed. "So you left me with a book full of events where my fortune cookies had turned up. It interested me, and to be honest freaked me out enough, for me to come and join you for breakfast this morning."

"Where I got you to open one of the eight fortune cookies that I had collected over the last few years," Peter said.

"Which told us to look at the first page of Peter's book, which in turn led us to Rachel who, to our surprise, already knew we were coming."

"Because," said Rachel joining in, "I had been given a fortune cookie of my own the night before that told me to be on the lookout for strangers needing help to solve a mystery."

"And that was pretty much the point I stopped thinking this was all just a coincidence," I admitted.

Rachel nodded her head in agreement and Peter smiled. Rachel continued the tale.

"So next you guys got me to pick one of the cookies and that led us to Little Dorrit Park, where we found poor Mr Fairchild."

"And Fairchild," Peter said picking the story up again, "led us to Terry Taylor."

"Who had also received one of my cookies from his Nan only that week, which led him to telling his grandfather a secret. Which we convinced him to tell us, and," I let out a sigh, "it proved to be somewhat anticlimactic."

Peter snorted.

"That's an understatement. The kid bumped into his Nan's ex-husband, and because he knows they don't get on he decided to keep it to himself. Someone alert the media."

We all fell silent again. Once more I was the one to break it.

"So what do we do now?"

We all exchanged glances. Peter blew out a breath.

"I have no idea," He admitted. "I feel like I'm trying to do a puzzle where someone's stolen the box lid."

I raised an eyebrow.

"Isn't that kind of your job?"

Peter rolled his eyes.

"Ha, bloody, ha. Yes, but in my day job most of the cases I investigate have the decency to obey all the laws of physics."

"But can't we approach it like a normal case?" asked Rachel. "Follow the clues, interview the witnesses, rough up some petty criminals."

"Oi," said Peter with mock offence, "I'll have you know that official Met policy requires us to refer to it as 'vigorous interrogation'."

Rachel held up her hands.

"I stand corrected. But my point still stands."

Peter took a slurp of his coke.

"You're right, normally that is exactly what we would do, and it's what I've been trying to do. I'd really like to talk to Mr Fairchild, see if he can tell us anything that would help, but that's not on the table right now, and to be honest I'm not sure it would be much help to us anyway."

"Why not?" I asked.

"Because I don't see how all this connects. At best he will be able to tell us who attacked him, which immediately takes it out of our hands and makes it part of the official investigation into his assault. Us tracking down Terry was probably a bit too close to interfering with an ongoing investigation as it is. If we try and find whoever it was that attacked Fairchild we will definitely be stepping on someone's toes and believe you me coppers don't appreciate that."

"So we follow the clues," said Rachel.

"What clues are those?" Peter asked. "I mean so far all we have done is go with our gut, there haven't been any real clues that we have put together using sound deductive reasoning and logic. We've just opened a cookie, read the message and guessed at what it meant."

"And it's worked," I put in.

"Yes, it's worked, but where has it led us?"

"It led us to Terry," said Rachel. "It led us to his, admittedly, underwhelming secret."

"Exactly and where does that leave us?"

I looked over at Rachel who met my gaze. Neither of us had any idea.

"Thank you," said Peter throwing up his hands, "you make my point perfectly."

"So why don't we open another cookie?" said Rachel, gesturing towards the plastic Tesco bag that now sat on the table.

"No," Peter and I said in unison.

Rachel's eyebrows went up.

"Ok, but why not?"

I looked at Peter hoping he would answer but he remained silent. I looked back at Rachel. I wasn't entirely sure how to explain because I didn't really understand it myself. As I struggled to put it into words I realised that Peter had already done so that morning.

"We've had our turn," I said simply. "It would be wrong, somehow, I have no idea why."

Rachel looked at me for a moment. Then she nodded.

"I know. I feel the same way. I was kind of hoping you didn't. It's like, I believe, no I know it would help us, but opening another one would, oh I don't know, violate the rules or something."

"Yeah," I said, "that's actually how Peter described it to me. It's like there are hidden rules, laws even, governing how all this works and we are somehow all aware of them simply by virtue of having opened the cookies and read the fortunes. If one of us opens another one that would somehow break the rules, and that feels like a bad idea to me."

Rachel's forehead crinkled slightly.

"But wait, I've actually opened three cookies. There was the one that saved Daniel Phillips' life, the one I opened last night, and the one you gave me earlier. So if there is some hidden rule about only being allowed to open one how did that work?"

"I've been thinking about that," said Peter. "I think the rules, if that's what we are calling them, only allow for the opening of one fortune per person."

Rachel opened her mouth to interrupt but Peter held up a finger.

"And yes, you have opened more than one, but I don't think you were the intended recipient for two of them. The first one was clearly meant to go to Mr Phillips; Rachel was just part of the delivery mechanism. And I think the same thing applies to the one we got you to open this morning Rachel, I think that one was, in a roundabout way, meant for Mr Fairchild."

"Wait, are you saying that the fortune wanted him to go to the park and get attacked?"

Peter shrugged.

"Maybe, though I don't think so. Maybe instead it wanted to make sure that we were there to help him after he did. As far as I can tell each fortune helps out one person in a specific time of need. Now I'd always sort of assumed that the person who opened the cookie was the one the message would help, but we know that's not true, because you opened the one that helped Mr Phillips. Well, you also opened the one that helped Mr Fairchild; neither was meant for you, only the one you opened last night. The one fortune per person rule stands."

Rachel frowned.

"But in what way did my fortune help me out in my time of need?"

"It got you to talk to us," I suggested.

Rachel smiled.

"I'm not that hard up for friends that I need magic cookies to help me meet people."

"Maybe your time of need hasn't happened yet," Peter said.

We both looked at him.

"Great," said Rachel, "there's something to look forward to."

"But," I said, "we all agree that none of us should open any more, at least not any of these ones."

"So," said Rachel with a shrug, "we get someone else to open one, heck we could ask someone right now."

I frowned at this.

"But who? I don't think we can give one to any old person who happens to walk by. The cookies seem, oh what's the right word, intended for people, they affect people's lives, they protect them. I'm not sure we can just have anyone open one, it has to be the right person, the person who was meant to get the cookie."

The other two looked at me and I suddenly felt a little foolish. I believed what I had said was true, though I have no idea how I knew that, but saying it out loud like that sounded a little crazy even to me. But neither Peter nor Rachel said anything and from the looks on their faces I could tell that they felt the same way about this issue. Even though we didn't know who they were for we did know that the remaining five cookies were in fact for specific people. It had felt right to give one to Fairchild, even though he was yet to open it, and what was more it had felt instinctual. I had known I was meant to give him one, and I felt certain I would know when we met someone else intended to receive one.

"How about Mrs Thompson?" Rachel suggested.

I thought about it for a moment. It seemed that in some point in the past she had received a cookie of her own, but she had never opened it and eventually it had found its way to Terry, who I believed was its intended recipient. She was connected to all this, it would make sense to give her one of the remaining cookies, and yet something made me hold back.

"I don't know why, but no, I don't think we can give one to her," I said haltingly.

"Why not?" asked Rachel.

I looked over at the Tesco bag.

"They're not meant for her, I don't know why," I said.

"Well great, so we are back to having no idea what to do. That's just awesome."

She reached into her coat pocket and pulled out her phone.

"Shit, I've been out for ages. If we don't have a plan of what to do, then I really need to get back to work."

There was more silence and more exchanged glances.

"Ok," said Rachel, "can you drive me back to work?"

Peter sighed, downed the rest of his drink and stood up.

"Come on."

Rachel and I followed him out of the canteen and headed back for the entrance. As we did so I heard a sudden clamour of noise from up the corridor we had walked down earlier to take Terry to see his

Nan. I paused and looked in the direction of the sound to see several people in blue scrubs hurrying further down the corridor and disappearing into a room on the right at the far end. Without realising it I found myself first walking and then running towards them. I passed the waiting room just as Terry opened the door and stuck his head out to see what was going on.

"Hey," he yelled as I sprinted past, "what's going on, why you running?"

I didn't answer because I didn't really know. I reached the room and threw myself into the doorway, slamming open a door that was in the process of being closed. To a guy who spends most of his days sitting in a quiet little room either working on a computer or at an easel accompanied only by a sleeping dog and occasional visits from a cat the room before me appeared to be in absolute chaos. People were shouting instructions and information back and forth and moving around in a way that seemed to me both perfectly synchronised and haphazard at the same time. I spotted Dr Hanson, apparently conducting the madness, and then I saw Mr Fairchild, lying in the bed, a thick bandage wrapped around his head and, if the commotion and the noise coming from the machines beside his bed were any indicator, busy dying.

"Gramps," came a cry from my side as Terry reached the door.

One of the nurses turned and gave us a stern

look.

"You can't be in here," she said.

I stepped back and she grabbed the door and closed it in our faces. The last thing I saw before it shut fully was Dr Hanson pressing the resuscitation paddles to Fairchild's chest.

"Clear!"

16

"Visions from the past can give us the keys to the present."
The Wisdom of Zhu Zhuang, No. 754

I stood there in shock, staring at the closed door. I couldn't believe this was happening again. I felt my stomach suddenly heave and I staggered backwards, only just managing to keep my burger and chips from making a reappearance.

"What's going on," demanded Terry, "what the fuck's going on?"

I turned to face him, but he seemed to be twisting and tilting from side to side. I felt my legs give way and all at once I was sitting on the floor.

"Hey, what's wrong with you?" he asked, but his voice seemed a very long way away.

I tried to look up at him, but my head felt heavy, way too heavy, and I sagged forward, trying to fight the dizziness that was threatening to overwhelm me.

"Not again," someone said using my voice.

I managed to turn my eyes to face the door as the memories flooded back with the force of a tsunami. A picture formed in my mind in vivid technicolour of Dr Hanson standing there, paddles in hand, just as he now stood beside Fairchild, only in my mind's eye he was standing beside Laci's bed. Her hospital gown had been pulled open revealing her nakedness beneath and I'd wanted to rush in and cover her up, knowing how embarrassed she would be to be seen like that by all the people crammed into her room. Like Fairchild her head, bald as a result of the chemo and surgery, had been heavily bandaged and she'd been similarly connected up to all manner of machines. I'd tried to force my way to her, but strong arms had held me back. Dr Hanson called a single word that didn't make it past the roaring of blood in my ears and Laci's entire body lurched violently. Now I'd seen pretty much every episode of ER, and Laci had always been a fan of Casualty and Holby City, so I'd fully understood what was happening on an intellectual level, but right at that moment I had wanted to kill Dr Hanson for hurting her like that and if not for the two people physically holding me back I probably would have thrown myself across the room at him. I remembered them dragging me outside, more people hurrying up to calm me down, and the door closing, cutting me off from the love of my life at the very moment when I felt she needed me most.

"Steve," said a voice beside me, "are you ok? If you can hear me the squeeze my hands."

A dark blur swam before my eyes and slowly resolved itself into a strong but worried face. I looked down and found that Peter was holding one of my hands in his and after a confused moment I managed to give it a squeeze. Peter smiled.

"Good, that's good mate. Rachel's gone to get someone. I think you fainted."

I looked at him and as I felt myself starting to come back to the present the tears came.

"It's happening again," I wept, "it's happening all over again."

Peter looked at me, obvious confusion on his face at my reaction.

"It's ok mate, the doctors are on it, Mr Fairchild is in good hands."

"No," I said clutching at his shirt, "you don't understand, this is what happened before, this is what happened to Laci."

Understanding entered Peter's eyes and with it his expression took on a level of compassion I wouldn't have thought possible from him.

"It's ok mate, I do understand. I get moments like

this too, they sneak up on you when you're not expecting it, knock the wind right out of you. Believe me, I am not enjoying being back in a hospital any more than you are, and Chris recovered, I can't imagine how much worse this all is for you."

I knew he was trying to help, heck on one level he was, but I could feel my anger building and I reached up and grabbed at his coat.

"You don't understand, it's him, Hanson, he was there when Laci died and now he's here, in there with Fairchild. Don't you see, it can't be a coincidence, not today, not with everything else that's happened, it just can't."

"What are saying?" came a sharp female voice. "Are you suggesting that the doctor is hurting my Douglas?"

I lifted my head and through my teary eyes I could see Irene Thompson standing there with the bearing of a soldier on parade, save that one of her arms was wrapped protectively around the shoulder of her grandson who looked scared out of his mind. I opened my mouth to speak but the words died in my throat. In the face of her stoic gaze my terror and certainty that Dr Hanson was somehow hurting rather than helping Mr Fairchild just collapsed, only to be replaced with doubt, embarrassment, and bone deep sorrow. I crumpled, folding in on myself, my head in my hands, my shoulders shaking as I wept silently.

"I, I don't know," I managed to say, "I'm sorry, I, I was sure, I thought, I don't know."

At that moment Rachel came running up with a broad-shouldered woman in hospital scrubs and together they and Peter helped me into a chair that I didn't recall seeing before. The nurse checked me over, asked me some questions that I answered and immediately forgot, and then gave me instructions as to what to do if I started feeling dizzy again. She did it all calmly, kindly and with a slightly dull tone of voice that spoke of routine and I immediately got the feeling I wasn't the first person to have some sort of breakdown in the face of a sudden cardiac event.

I looked over at the four worried people standing in the corridor. Rachel had a hand up to her mouth and looked as though she might be biting the side of one of her fingers as she looked at me with a mix of concern, alarm, and not a little bit of fear. Seeing as she had known me for no more than a couple of hours she had no idea what to make of my reaction, and I suspected she was once again questioning her involvement in this whole thing. Peter was also looking my way, hands in the pockets of his coat, a stern but concerned expression on his face. Peter was a kindred spirit, we had both walked the same path, and though he had not travelled as far as me he well knew the toll it could take on a person. But even so he seemed taken aback by the strength of my reaction and the flicker of doubt that I could see in his eyes was well and truly aimed at my involvement in this investigation rather than his own.

Behind these two relative strangers, who I none the less found myself considering as friends, stood Terry, looking younger than ever, and the iron lady that was Irene Thompson. Their attention was well and truly focused on the door to the room in which their loved one was currently fighting for his life, though Irene did take a moment to flash a disapproving glare in my direction. I closed my eyes and concentrated on my breathing for a bit. I also thought over what I had said to Peter about Dr Hanson being here. Was there something to it, or after a day of chasing the impossible was I seeing predestination where only coincidence, genuine, honest to God, coincidence was to be found? I didn't know any more and despite the certainty I had expressed over lunch I found myself suddenly questioning everything that had happened that day. What was I doing running around all over London in pursuit of some intangible something that less that twenty-four hours earlier I would have declared, with all the force of science and logic on my side, was nothing but mumbo jumbo claptrap. Had I made a massive mistake? Were my first thoughts about Peter's mental health accurate and somehow he had dragged first me and then Rachel into his delusion? Hell, for that matter could I even trust Rachel herself? What if she was in on it? It had been Peter's book that led us to her, and I only had their words for it that they had not met before. For all I knew they could be old friends and be working together on one of those super villain plans of Machiavellian proportions that Peter seemed so concerned about. With what end? To drive me crazy, to make me doubt the nature of reality, to cause me to have a complete nervous breakdown?

"Jesus," I hissed beneath my breath, "don't go down that path again. The world isn't out to get you for fuck's sake."

When Laci had died I kind of lost myself a bit. I'd somehow not realised how profoundly foundational she had become to my life. Laci, my wonderful Laci, so beautiful, smart, kind, funny, passionate, forthright, determined, stubborn, pig-headed, and annoyingly right far more often than I was. She always had time for others, occasionally to her own detriment, couldn't cook for shit, and would turn from an Amazonian warrior capable of calmly facing down one of her clients in the midst of a full on mental breakdown into a blubbering child at the merest hint of a spider. She was the light that showed me the way, the source of both my greatest happiness and biggest frustrations, and the part of me I'd never known I was missing until we met. And then she was gone, and my foundation crumbled.

I became convinced that her death couldn't have been a natural event. Something so monumental, so earth shattering, so devastating to the very fundamental fabric of the universe, just couldn't be an average, normal, everyday thing that happened to hundreds of thousands of people every year. It had to be more than that, there had to be some deeper meaning to it all, and by God I became determine to prove it. I'd been a right dick to the hospital, insisting upon investigations and police involvement and that they tear the whole goddamned place apart until they could point me to the people, because it had to be bigger than any one person, responsible. At that point in time if someone had been found to have caused Laci's death in some way I have little doubt I would have killed them, and I have never been a violent man, never even been in a real fight, unless you count Timothy Wheeler when I was seven. But during those few months immediately following her death I was not myself, I was a new creature born of grief, and sorrow, and rage beyond measure. The Steve Lander that Laci knew died the same day she did, and the man who now sat in a hospital corridor desperately trying to hold it all together was a mere shadow of the person who had lived before.

If I hadn't fallen asleep in front of the TV one night and awoken to find one of those competitive baking shows on the screen I am not sure what would have happened. The contestants on the show were making fortune cookies and I'd found the whole process fascinating. I'd always enjoyed baking and, though I hadn't really done any since Laci got sick, as I sat there watching that show I had been overcome with a desire to break out my rolling pin and apron once more. I had spent the rest of the night baking batch after batch of fortune cookies until I was able to produce something that came close to my exacting standards. I had then staggered up to the bedroom and fallen asleep fully clothed, only to start again in the morning. I had thrown everything I was feeling into those cookies, all the pain and anger that was constantly threatening to erupt out of me, as well as all of the profound joy and love that I'd felt for my wife and which had only grown stronger with every day that we had spent together, and which showed no sign of stopping in its upward trajectory simply because she was no longer there by my side.

I had set out to make the best fortune cookies it was possible to make. Once I had perfected my recipe I had turned my attention to the fortunes themselves. I had invested all the artistic skill I possessed into making those tiny bits of one centimetre by five velum the very best they could possibly be. I had treated the whole thing with the seriousness and dedication that I prided myself in bringing to my architecture jobs. I did mountains of unnecessary research, sourced the very best materials, and set myself to writing the fortunes themselves with a clarity of mind that would have made a Buddhist monk jealous. I don't think I am bragging when I say that I succeeded in my aim. My cookies had taken first place in a county wide baking competition, and soon after the orders had started to come in from restaurants all over the country. People didn't seem to be able to get enough of them. If I'd had any sense I would have started a business, hired in some people and churned them out by the thousand. But as it was I insisted on making every batch personally and alone. Besides I think the secret ingredient in each batch may have been a piece of my soul, and I am not sure that would have scaled to industrial levels.

Making those cookies had probably saved my life, or at the very least stopped me from doing something that I would have regretted for the rest of it. They brought me a sense of calm, like the eye of the hurricane that my life had become. They let me think, let me forget, and yet at the same time let me feel close to Laci. And now they had led me here. Back to a hospital. Back to Dr Hanson.

As I thought his name, as if summoned from my mind, the door to Fairchild's room opened and Hanson stepped out into the corridor. He looked ruffled; his scrubs slightly askew, his usually perfectly neat hair a mess and yet somehow still perfect, and a sheen of sweat coating his forehead. But despite this he was smiling, a full on, hundred watt, leading actor's smile.

"We got him back," he said in triumph.

And in that moment I knew.

17

"A tall dark stranger will come into your life."
The Wisdom of Zhu Zhuang, No. 7

Rachel let out a whoop. Terry started to laugh and cry at the same time. Peter closed his eyes and whispered something that might have been a prayer of thanks under his breath, and Irene simply nodded, smiled, and shook the doctor's hand, though her grip on her grandson's shoulder tightened so much that I saw him shrug it off with a pained expression.

"It was touch and go there for a moment," Hanson was explaining, "but we have a great team here at King's, and we weren't about to give up on him."

"Thank you doctor," Irene said, her voice steady but the joy evident none the less. "I don't know what I would have done without him. You are a Godsend."

Hanson nodded politely in grudging acceptance of the praise and then his face grew serious for a moment.

"Now you must understand that he is not out of the woods yet, we will be monitoring him closely for the next twenty-four hours. However, if he makes it until this time tomorrow without any further complications then I genuinely expect him to make a full recovery."

Irene took a breath and pulled herself up straight, or at least straighter.

"I understand doctor; can we go see him now?"

"He's asleep again, and I would like you to leave him that way for the time being. But I see no reason why you can't be with him while he's resting. It will be nice for him to see a familiar face when he wakes up."

Irene thanked him again and she and Terry moved into the room where I could see Fairchild, eyes closed, but still very much alive, laying on the bed. Hanson looked into the room for a few seconds himself before the door was closed and he turned to face Peter, Rachel, and me, his smile still in place, but now holding more of a quiet contentment than the radiant joy it had been filled with mere moments before. He looked around and saw me sitting in the chair and his expression immediately became one of concern.

"Mr Lander, are you ok? If you don't mind me saying you look rather awful."

I didn't answer, I just stared up at him.

"He had, umm, well he had a bit of a moment when things were all kicking off back there," Peter explained. "But I think he's doing alright now, aren't you Steve?"

I turned my eyes to Peter and after a moment forced myself to nod.

"Yes," I managed to force out, "I'm doing alright, just a bad memory, you understand don't you Dr Hanson?"

Hanson was quiet for a moment and nodded.

"Of course, this must be very traumatic for you. I have no doubt it has brought back lots of memories I am sure you would have rather kept forgotten."

"Oh I've never forgotten," I said softly. "But yes, it did bring back a few things."

Hanson's eyes met mine for a moment before he took a deep breath and the smile, perhaps a bit forced this time, returned.

"Well, I am glad you are doing alright. If you start to feel bad again please be sure to speak to one of the nurses. Now, if you will excuse me I have other patients to see to. No rest for the wicked and all that."

And with this he flashed his smile at Peter and

Rachel, gave me one more look, and turned and headed off down the corridor at what seemed to me an accelerated pace.

"Bastard," I hissed through my teeth, too quiet for anyone to hear.

Once Hanson was out of sight Peter let out an exaggerated sigh.

"Well, that was all a bit too exciting," he said, with a weak smile.

"I know," agreed Rachel, "I thought poor Mr Fairchild was a goner for sure, and Steve, you scared the life out of me. I mean what the hell was that all about?"

"Sorry," I said. "As Hanson said, it brought back some painful memories and I kind of freaked out for a bit there."

Peter nodded.

"It can all be a bit much coming to a place like this at the best of times. But if you've had a bad experience in the past it can be even worse. Believe me mate, I get where you're coming from on this."

I gave him a nod of my own.

"Yeah, but hey I'm better now, I feel, well I feel clearer, if that makes any sense."

Peter's eyebrows went up a little at this, as if he were trying to puzzle out what I meant, and then he just seemed to accept it.

"Sure, that's good to hear."

"It really is," agreed Rachel as she pulled out her phone and looked at the screen, "but now I need to get back to work more than ever, so if we're still at an impasse can we get back to giving me a lift?"

"You're right," I said. "We have taken up enough of your time today. Maybe something else will come up that will help us out. But right now we should get you back to the shop, and don't worry, we will tell Rob it's our fault you were out so long."

Rachel waved her hand in a dismissive gesture.

"Oh don't worry about him, he knows I bring more money into the shop than anything else, I won't be in that much trouble. I just don't want to take the piss, you know."

I nodded and struggled to stand up. Peter reached out and offered me a hand. I thanked him and the three of us stood in a circle, much like we had done outside Rachel's bookshop. None of us spoke and I started to get an uneasy feeling in my stomach.

"This kind of feels like an end," I said.

"I know what you mean," said Rachel, "I feel like this is a special day and that if we leave it, if we put it aside and start afresh tomorrow well, things won't be as special."

"Sometimes it is best to take a break from a case so that you can have a fresh take on it in the morning," Peter said.

Rachel and I looked at him and he held up his hands.

"Alright, I feel it too, but what are we meant to do? We can't make something happen, and short of us opening more of the cookies, which we all agreed not to do, I am not sure how we can get more leads."

I reached into my pocket and pulled out the bag containing the remaining cookies. I opened it and looked inside shaking my head.

"What is it about these things that makes me certain they hold the answer, and yet equally as certain that we can't just open them all to find it out?"

"I think it's because the cookies are only one part of the equation," said Peter. "The cookies need to be opened by the right person for it to make sense. Take Rachel for instance. If anyone other than her had received that message there is a very good chance we would have ended up going to a different park. Mr Fairchild might well have lain there for another hour or so before someone found him, hell he may well have died before help could have arrived."

He shrugged.

"I think it really is as simple as that. If the cookies are not opened by the right person the message will either be meaningless or misunderstood. We all know that, on some instinctive level, and, well this might sound stupid, I feel like a prat saying it, but I think there might be, well, forces at work, I'm not sure how else to explain why we all feel the same about so many different things."

"So," I said drawing the word out, "are you

saying you think we should call it a day and see what happens? See if these forces do anything else."

He shrugged, as I knew he would.

"I really don't know what else we can do. Everything that has happened today has felt right, every step of the way the path has been laid out there for us to follow, and not once did I have any doubt that we were heading in the right direction. I think that when we find ourselves back on that path we will know it."

I nodded.

"Agreed. The funny thing is I have this feeling that I know where all this will end, but I feel that we still have a few miles left to travel before we can get there."

Peter raised an eyebrow at this.

"Care to share?"

I shook my head.

"It's nothing, just a crazy thought that popped into my head when I was lying on the floor having a panic attack. It's more than likely nothing, it wouldn't be the first time my brain has played tricks on me. But hey, who knows. What's that old saying, just because you have grief induced paranoia it doesn't mean they aren't out to get you."

I smiled to show I was joking but the other two gave me slightly worried looks.

"Forget it, come on, let's get Rachel back to work."

We headed down the corridor in silence. None of

us wanted to head back outside without a next destination in mind, but what else could we do. We'd lost our map and while I had an idea of where we might be heading our actual destination could be somewhere else entirely. Hell, there was still a chance this was all one big coincidence and we'd all turned into Jim Carrey's character from the film *The Number 23*, running around the city chasing something that wasn't really there and yet seeing clues to it everywhere. I shook my head, chuckling slightly to myself at the idea and glanced down at the plastic bag in my hand and for the first time that day actually thought about the sanity of using fortune cookies to make your decisions.

And because I wasn't paying attention I rounded the corner and walked straight into someone. The plastic bag when flying from my hand and I staggered back a pace.

"I'm sorry, I didn't see you," I said in a rush.

The tall, handsome black man had an annoyed expression on his face, but he took a deep breath and brought his anger under control.

"It's alright," he said, "these things happen. I wasn't really looking where I was going either."

As he spoke I found that I recognised him, though I knew for a fact we had never met before. It took me a moment to place why he seemed so familiar, but then it occurred to me. It was because I had seen the various aspects of his face before, spread across the faces of Irene Thompson and

Terry Taylor.

"Are you Mr Taylor, Terry's dad?"

He gave me a suspicious look but before he could answer the short, dark haired, white woman at his side, who I simply hadn't noticed until that moment, spoke first.

"How do you know my Terry?"

"We brought him here to see his grandfather," Peter said. "I'm DI Fuller; this is Mr Lander and Miss Jones."

"Right," said Mrs Taylor, "well thank you, we appreciate it."

I smiled slightly at this, once again impressed at how so many problems seemed to go away when Peter mentioned that he was a police officer. I am pretty sure that things would have turned out somewhat differently if it had just been me and Rachel who had picked up their son and driven him to the hospital. I am pretty sure that the Taylors would have had some serious questions for us about that.

"Terry and his Nan are at the end of the hall with Mr Fairchild," Rachel explained. "I am sure they will be glad to see you, they've been through a lot."

Mr Taylor nodded his thanks at this and Mrs Taylor put a hand to her mouth and looked worried. We moved aside so they could pass and they started to move down the corridor. I looked down at the floor where I had dropped the bag to find that it had split and its contents were spilt out across the floor. I bent down to pick up the cookies, concerned that I could only see three of them, when I heard Mrs Taylor's voice.

"Excuse me, but I think these are yours."

I looked up to see Mr and Mrs Taylor standing there, each holding one of my cookies in their outstretched hand. I felt my face break into a smile. I knew, without a shadow of a doubt, that we had just found the map again.

"No," I said standing up, "I am pretty sure they are yours."

18

"The words of strangers will set you on the path to a new destination."
The Wisdom of Zhu Zhuang, No. 612

Mr Taylor, whose name was Mark, looked interested but sceptical, while his wife, Anna, stared at us as though we had horns growing out the top of our heads.

"Magic fortune cookies?" she said.

"Well," I said, "that's not what we've been calling them."

"Ok, what have you been calling them?"

I swallowed.

"Umm, psychic fortune cookies," I said lamely.

"Right," Anna said, drawing out the word, "well I'm glad we cleared that up, because that's totally different to magic fortune cookies, I wouldn't want to mix the two up."

Rachel took a step forward.

"Look, I know how all this sounds, believe me we all do, but these cookies are the reason we found Douglas in that park, probably the reason he is still alive now. They led us to him."

Anna eyed Rachel up and down, taking in the Madam Josephine costume beneath her puffer jacket. I could tell that she didn't consider Rachel the most credible of witnesses when it came to matters of the supernatural. Strangely people dressed as fortune tellers don't come across as entirely unbiased on the matter.

"Couldn't all this just be a coincidence?" Mark cut in. "I mean strange events like this happen, it doesn't mean there is anything paranormal going on."

I smiled.

"You sound like I did yesterday evening. But since then I've seen way too many coincidences lining up in just the right way for me not to think that there is something, some guiding force behind it all."

"Are you religious Mrs Taylor?" Peter asked, speaking for the first time since we had started trying to fill them in on what had been going on that day.

Anna reached up and touched the small silver cross hanging around her neck.

"Yes," she said, her tone ever so slightly defensive, "but I don't see what that has to do with all this."

"I've never been a big believer myself," Peter went on, "my wife is the one with all the faith. I guess being a police officer can make you have doubts about the existence of a God who loves us watching over everything. But I have read my Bible, and I clearly remember at least two things from it. First it tells us that God has his eye is upon all of us, and on sparrows apparently, and secondly that he works in mysterious ways."

"Yes, but I am pretty sure there is nothing in the Bible about magic, sorry psychic fortune cookies."

Peter shrugged.

"Maybe not, but God did deliver messages by way of burning bushes, blinding lights and talking animals, so who are we to say what he would and wouldn't do. All I know is that one of these cookies saved my son's life, absolutely no question about it. Another saved a woman named Emma Billing from being assaulted, another stopped a man named Daniel Phillips from dying of a nut allergy, and this very morning one of these magic psychic fortune cookies led a man with first aid experience to a small park where someone you care about was in desperate need of him."

He smiled.

"Like I said, I am not much of a believer, but if you can't see the hand of God in all that well, as far as I am concerned, you're just not paying attention."

Anna drew in a deep breath at this and I could see that Peter's words had touched her deeply. I looked over at Peter. This was the first time he had mentioned anything about God and I wondered whether he actually believed it or was simply saying so for Anna's sake.

"Ok," Anna said with a sigh, "I guess if he wanted to God could do all that, it makes more sense to me than magic or psychic powers anyway. But I am still not sure why you're giving these to us."

She held up the fortune cookie she had picked up from the floor.

"Because you are meant to have them," I said. "And no, don't ask us how we know, we just do. Hell I'm not sure I believe in any kind of God at all, though I will admit to having done more than my fair share of praying in recent years, but if he does exist I can accept the idea that he could make it so we would know who the cookies should go to. I mean if Amazon can get millions of deliveries to the right place every year then I am sure the creator of the universe can get a few fortune cookies to the right people once in a while, right?"

I looked back and forth between Anna and her husband, watching their faces, the confusion, the re-evaluation of deeply held beliefs, and the beginnings of acceptance.

"And what's more," I ventured, "I think you believe it as well."

Almost in unison they both looked down at the cookies in their hands and then at each other.

"So," asked Mark, "what now? Do we just open them?"

I held up my hands.

"Honestly, I have no idea, but I am pretty sure you should do what you think is right. Open them, or don't, maybe give them to someone else. At this point I am willing to believe that whatever force is behind this, be it God or something else, it knows what it is doing and whatever you decide to do will be the right thing. So go with your gut."

The two of them stood there in silence for a moment before Anna opened her shoulder bag and dropped her cookie inside, while Mark, staring at his for a few moments longer, reached up with his other hand and started to unwrap it. The three of us leant forward expectantly, while Anna went back to looking at us as if we were crazy people, something for which an argument could definitely be made. We watched as Mark untied the bow and peeled back the wrapping. He took the cookie out, stuffing the now empty wrapper into a pocket in the same movement, and broke the cookie in two.

"Am I meant to eat it?" he asked, holding the half without the fortune up before his mouth.

"Up to you," I said. "Though I can't speak for

how fresh it will be."

Mark looked at the piece of fortune cookie in his hand, shrugged, and, just as his son had done with his old cookie, popped it into his mouth. He chewed for a bit then nodded.

"Hmm, not bad," he said.

He removed the fortune from the other half of the cookie and ate that half as well. I don't know about the others but I had to bite my tongue to stop myself from hurrying him up. Finally he looked at the fortune and a puzzled expression appeared on his face. He looked up at us and held up the fortune.

"Do you want me to read it to you?" he asked.

"Yes," all three of us said in unison.

"Ok, ok, but I think you guys are all taking this a little too seriously."

He sniffed, cleared his throat, and adjusted the fortune before his eyes as if he were having difficulty seeing it. It was all I could do not to rip it out of his hands.

"So, umm, it says it doesn't matter how old you get the place you grew up will always feel like home," He turned the fortune over in his hands. "No lucky numbers?"

I closed my eyes for a moment at that.

"No, just the fortune," I said. "And does it mean anything to you?"

Mark thought for a moment then shook his head.

"Not really, was it meant to?"

I felt myself deflated slightly, but thankfully

Peter stepped in to take up the questioning.

"Thinking about what the fortune said, where do you think it's referring to?"

"That's easy enough I guess, the place I grew up that still feels like home would be my mum's house."

"And would that be the place she lives now? The place she shares with Mr Fairchild."

Mark nodded.

"Yeah, she's been in that house for years, pretty much raised me there single handed after my father walked out on us."

I saw a quick flash of remembered childhood pain in his eyes as he said this to which I could easily relate. My own parents had divorced when I was young and my father had moved to Australia with, yeah you guessed it, his secretary. I had no idea if he was still there, or if they were still together, and I didn't much care either way for the matter. My mother had never remarried and, much like Irene had done with Mark, had raised me pretty much on her own after that. She'd been a good mum in her own way, but had been emotionally damaged by the actions of my father and as a result had not been the most forthcoming when it came to offering affections. She had died after a fairly short struggle with cancer when I was in my mid-twenties leaving me alone, or at least I would have been alone if it were not for Laci, her brother Darren, and her wonderful parents.

"And of course eventually Doug moved in," Mark said drawing my attention back to him, "got to be getting on for fourteen ago years now. I'd only been moved out a handful of years myself, and Anna was pregnant with Terry at the time, so yeah, got to be almost fourteen years. Man, time flies doesn't it."

Peter smiled.

"It does indeed," he agreed. "But you're sure; the fortune's talking about Mrs Thompson's house?"

Mark smiled a little at this.

"I'm not entirely sure that the fortune is talking about anything at all, but yeah, sure, if it is talking about anything it would be my mum's house. So what does that mean?"

Peter shrugged.

"Not sure yet, but it gives us a place to start, which is something we didn't have a moment ago, so thank you."

Mark glanced at the fortune again then back at us.

"Sure, whatever. Look, as interesting and weird as this has all been we really need to get on and see if Doug is doing alright if that's ok with you?"

Peter raised a hand in a 'go right ahead' gesture.

"Please, go be with your family. And thank you for taking the time to help us out."

Mark gave a weak smile and Anna rolled her eyes.

"Sure, umm, good luck with whatever it is you

are doing and, yeah, thanks for helping Doug out like that. He's technically my step-dad, but he's always been there for me ever since he started seeing my mum you know, and as far as Terry is concerned Doug is his grandfather, he's certainly a better one than my actual dad has ever been to him. He would have been devastated had anything more serious happened to him, we all would."

Peter nodded.

"I understand, I'm just glad I was there to help."

There was an awkward pause and before Mark reached out and gave Peter's hand a quick shake.

"So, yeah, thanks. See you."

Anna gave us all a wary smile and the two of them moved off down the corridor. They had made it all of three steps when Rachel called out after them.

"Wait, there's something you need to know."

Mark and Anna turned but they didn't step back towards us.

"What is it?" Mark asked.

Rachel glanced over at Peter and I and from her expression I could tell that she was already doubting her decision.

"If it's what I think you are going to say I think you should tell them. I mean it's hardly earthshattering is it?"

"Yeah, but we did promise to keep it secret," Rachel countered.

"I'm sure Terry will forgive us," said Peter. "And

I'm with Steve on this one, we should tell them."

"Seriously," Mark said, a slight trace of annoyance in his voice, "whatever it is either tell us or don't, but I really would like to go see my family now."

Rachel paused for a fraction of a second, still torn between saying what she thought they needed to know and the promise we had all made to Terry not to say anything. Mark shook his head and started to turn around again.

"Your father is back in town," Rachel blurted out. "Terry saw him."

"What?" Mark said turning back and this time stepping back towards us. "What did you say?"

Rachel tilted her head slightly.

"Terry told us that he saw your father, spoke to him even, a few days back."

"He did? But why didn't he tell us?"

"He said that knowing would just upset everyone and that he didn't like how people get when your father is around. So he decided to keep it to himself, until the other day at least when one of the fortune cookies told him to share his secret, and he told Douglas."

At this Mark and Anna turned to look at each other in horror.

"You don't think that Teddy could have…" Anna said, leaving the sentence unfinished.

Mark shook his head.

"No, I mean, I don't know."

He turned to face us again.

"Where did you find Doug again?"

"Little Dorrit Park," Peter answered, "Why?"

Mark turned away with a curse and Anna brought a hand to her mouth.

"What is it?" asked Peter again.

Anna shook her head and answered for her husband who suddenly seemed to be struggling to keep his anger under control.

"Strange as it seems but Little Dorrit Park was the place Irene and Teddy had their first kiss. Teddy has always said afterwards that it was his favourite place in the city. If that's where Doug got attacked and he knew that Teddy was back in town there is a good chance that he went looking for him there and that it was Teddy who hit him."

Mark turned back towards us, his jaw clenched tight and his hands balled into fists.

"My dad was always a violent man, used to beat my mum black and blue when I was a kid, me too as I got older. I said earlier that he left us, well that's not exactly true. He got banged up for aggravated assault, some guy looked at him funny," he made quote marks with his fingers, "in a pub and he just snapped. Anyway while he was inside mum divorced him and had a restraining order placed against him. He wasn't allowed within a hundred yards of us."

He looked off into the middle distance, as if seeing something that wasn't there.

"Of course he violated that as soon as he got out. I had to call the police on him myself. Mum ended up with a broken arm and he went back inside for another six months. Since then he shows up every so often, usually for events like birthdays, his and mum's wedding anniversary, that sort of thing, and whenever he does he causes one kind of trouble or another."

He shook his head as if trying to dismiss any connection to a man he obviously despised.

"Like Anna said, I'm also pretty sure that he's the one who hurt Doug given where it happened, he always hated him for being good to mum in a way he never could. And if that's the case he will know that he's going to end up in trouble sooner or later, and that makes him unpredictable and that's not good news."

"Any idea where he might be going now?" Peter asked his tone official.

Mark snorted.

"You could start with all the pubs in East London," he said clearly angry.

Then he took a breath and shook his head.

"Sorry, not your fault, but I have no idea."

"I know where he is," I said.

Everyone turned to face me.

"In fact," I said gesturing to the fortune Mark still held in his hand, "we all do."

19

"Home is the place you can always get a warm reception."
The Wisdom of Zhu Zhuang, No. 1104

"So, are you sure we are doing the right thing?" asked Mark, for what seemed like the fiftieth time in the last few minutes.

Peter, Rachel and I had all been certain that we needed to head to the house that Mark grew up in and still thought of as home post haste and after a moment's hesitation Mark had decided that he wanted to come with us. He had been second guessing himself ever since.

"Maybe I should have stayed with Anna," he

said, turning slightly in his seat to look back the way we had come.

We were back in Peter's car, this time with Mark in the passenger seat and Rachel and me in the rear, and were heading north east across the city towards Peckham as fast as London traffic would allow.

"We're not too far away now," said Peter, his eyes locked on the road. "It would take longer to drive you back than to get to the house. Let's go there, check the place out, and if everything is fine I will drive you straight back to the hospital."

Mark nodded to himself a few times and mumbled something under his breath that sounded like grudging agreement, but then this was the second time that he and Peter had had this exact conversation since we left the hospital, and as such I expected him to start complaining again at any minute. When we had first spoken to him and his wife at the hospital Mark had struck me as a confident, thoughtful and friendly man. However, since learning that his father was back in town all of that seemed to have fallen apart. Now he seemed to be constantly flipping back and forth between outright anger and cowering nervousness while at the same time being completely unable to stick with any decision he made. He seemed like a completely different person, almost as if the man had reverted back to the angry confused teenager he had been when his father had still been a prominent part of his life.

"Are you sure this is a good idea?" he asked after only a minute or so of not speaking. "I mean we are heading to my Mum's house because a fortune cookie said something about my childhood home. I'm no expert but this really doesn't feel like standard police procedure."

"Oh, you'd be surprised," said Peter. "I could tell you stories that would make this outing look like an average day on the job."

Mark turned and stared at him in obvious concern and after a few seconds Peter chuckled.

"Ok, yeah this is a bit out of the ordinary, I will grant you that, but so is everything else that has happened to us so far today, and that includes finding Mr Fairchild in that park."

He glanced quickly over at Mark and saw that he still looked far from convinced.

"Look, I've been looking into this fortune cookie thing for two years now, and every step of the way I have become more and more convinced that there is something to it. As crazy as it seems I really do believe that we are being guided by these things, that the fortunes, or whatever is behind them, wants to lead us somewhere."

He looked into the rear-view mirror and caught my eye for a second and when he spoke again I felt sure the words were mainly directed at me.

"I also believe that whatever they are leading us to is something big, something important. The events of today are over and above anything I have seen so far in the rest of my investigation. The sheer number of things that have happened today make it feel like things are coming to a head. I really believe that we are nearing the end of the road here. And right now," he glanced at Mark again, "that road is leading to Mrs Thompson's house."

Mark turned and looked out of the window, lapsing into silence again. It didn't last long.

"I really think I should have waited at the hospital."

"Well," said Peter, "too late now, we're here."

He flipped on his indicator and pulled up against the kerb. We parked up next to a three-storey estate building that stretched most of the length of the street. It reminded me in many ways of the London Bridge Station building that we had passed earlier in the day. It had that same appearance of something old that had recently been given a makeover and much of the brickwork was of a similar colour. Each level of the building represented a row of small flats with dozens of families living in close proximity. It was the kind of building you simply didn't see in the country, something unique to big cities like London. A mental picture of human sized sardine tins popped into my head and I was sure that if the designers of this and the other estate buildings that featured prominently in the area could have gotten away with it they would have probably gone for something along those lines. Lots of people crammed into as small an area as possible.

I clambered out of the car and looked up at the building. It was now mid-afternoon on a Saturday and it was clear that there were plenty of people in residence. I could hear music blaring from several open windows producing a cacophonic mixture of reggae, drum and bass, and harsh, angry rap that hung around the estate like a fog. I saw Peter wrinkle his nose and a moment later I picked up a faint whiff of marijuana drifting in the air, not that an upstanding citizen like myself would recognise such a thing of course. Looking around I saw that the George Cross flag hung everywhere, from windows and balconies and in one case on an actual flag pole. One flat towards the end of the block had even gone the extra step of hanging matching bunting. The overly patriotic display confused me at first until I remembered reading something about England making it to the finals of the European championship, or cup, or something like that. I looked over at Peter and pointed at the flags.

"They're a football thing right?" I asked.

Peter closed his eyes, shook his head and sighed in a single motion.

"Yes Steve, they're a football thing. Seriously, do you pay attention to anything other than baking?"

"Hey, I can predict the future remember, that puts a lot of pressure on a man's time."

Peter chuckled and I smiled. Mark however was not at all amused.

"Are we going to look at my mum's house or

not?" he asked. "I don't want to be here all day for nothing."

Peter gestured for Mark to lead on and he headed off to the right and with us all following dutifully along behind. All the flats on the ground floor of the estate building had small gardens out the front, though I use the word "garden" in the same way other parts of London use the word "park". A grassed area, the width of the flat and a couple of meters deep separated the flats from the pavement, and it seemed to me that many of the residents were involved in some sort of competition to see who could cram the most stuff onto that tiny piece of green land. Several of the flats contented themselves to just the mandatory collection of wheelie bins, black, brown, and blue, but others had accessorised with a wide variety of other objects. Garden gnomes were popular, as were potted plants. One house had a palm tree planted in the small area that reached up to the second storey, while someone else had decided to build a shed on their small patch of land. The flat that Mark led us to had, aside from the bins of course, only two small terracotta pots, both containing rose bushes, positioned to either side of the front door. They both looked well cared for, which having met Irene Thompson did not surprise me at all, but sadly neither were in bloom at this time of year.

Mark fumbled in his pocket and pulled out a set of keys, sorted through them and located a worn latch key. He slid the key into the lock, paused, and turned to look at us.

"I am sure this is all a massive waste of time."

We all nodded and smiled and reassured him that he was probably right, but that it was worth checking now that we were there, and finally he turned back to the door, unlocked it and pushed it open. The front door led into a small entry hall, barely big enough for two people, and Mark stopped there as soon as he got inside.

"I should probably get you to take your shoes off," he said. "Mum doesn't like shoes on the carpet."

"We will just take a quick look," assured Peter, "it should be fine."

Mark looked down at our feet, apparently evaluating them for cleanliness, before relenting.

"Alright, come in," he said, pushing open the door to his right that led into the house proper.

We followed in behind him, stepping through the hall and into what turned out to be the living room, and one by one came to an abrupt stop.

"Shit," said Rachel.

"What the hell?" said Mark.

Looking around I was tempted to add an invective of my own but I held my tongue. The place was trashed. Everything that could be, and some things that I would have thought couldn't, had been turned over, torn open, smashed up, and thrown about. Mark turned a slow circle taking it all in, an expression of growing horror on his face.

"Jesus, what has he done this time?"

"You think this was your father?" Peter asked.

"Who else," Mark snapped, "but he has really outdone himself this time. I mean he threw a brick through the window once, and I'm pretty sure he slashed Mum's tyres a year or so back, but this, this is something else."

Peter moved carefully forward, making sure not to step on anything.

"So he has targeted Mrs Thompson before."

Mark nodded.

"Several times, usually gets away with it as we can never really prove it, but who else could it have been. He has never moved on, never accepted that we don't want anything to do with him anymore."

"If you're right that it was him who attacked Mr Fairchild it makes me think that he is escalating. He probably knows he will be in serious trouble when we catch up with him and so had nothing to lose by coming here."

Mark walked over to another door, opened it and walked inside.

"God damn it, he's destroyed everything in here as well. He's smashed all of Mum's photos; she's gonna be heart broken."

Peter followed Mark through the door leaving me and Rachel in the living room.

"Should we try tidying up a bit?" she suggested.

"Maybe, I'd hate to have them come home to

this, not after everything they have been through."

"Leave it," Peter's voice sounded from the other room. "The investigating officers will want to see it as it is."

I glanced at Rachel, shrugged and headed towards the door at the far end of living room, leaving her looking around the living room and shaking her head sadly. The door was slightly ajar and through the gap I could see broken crockery, split cereal packets, and washing powder spread all over the white tiled floor. There was also a smell that I recognised but couldn't immediately place, and yet which struck me as strangely out of place. I pushed open the door and walked into the kitchen taking in the destruction. I was a few steps into the room when I looked up from the trashed floor to see a solid, angry looking black man glaring at me from a few worryingly short feet away.

It's funny the sort of things that go through your mind at times like this. On the drive over Mark had explained that his father Teddy was in his late sixties and as such I had formed an image in my head of a frail, greying man, angry at the world, a threat to someone like Fairchild, but nothing for a guy like me to worry about. In that moment I found myself remembering that Bruce Willis is in his sixties, and both Stallone and Arnie are in their seventies. Teddy Taylor definitely fit into this older action hero category rather than the typical pensioner group I had assigned him to. Even if I hadn't been told I would have known that Teddy was a violent man. He was muscled in the manner of a boxer, all upper body, broad shoulders, and thick neck. His nose had obviously been broken in the past, more than likely several times, and he kept his head low, forehead forward in a clear, challenging posture. The old adage about the dangers of a cornered animal sprang to mind, something that I imagined was especially true when the animal in question was a battle hardened wolf and you were very much a domestic dog, and pretty much a lap dog at that.

"And who the fuck are you?" he asked me in a harsh whisper.

I immediately wanted to turn and run, the anger in those six words making me seriously want to be somewhere else, but the sheer aggression in the man's expression froze me in place. It was only then that I noticed what he was holding in his large hands and all at once the smell I'd noticed made perfect sense.

"Shit," I said finally adding my invective to the situation.

"Is someone else in there Steve?" Peter called from the other room.

I opened my mouth but suddenly Teddy's finger was pointing in my direction.

"You say a fucking word and I will fucking kill you."

I swallowed, convinced not only that he would

but that he could. My eyes flicked down to his hand again and the green emergency petrol can he held there. Looking down at the ground I could see that there was a fairly large wet patch spreading out across the floor where he had already emptied some of the can's content onto the kitchen tiles.

"Steve?" Peter called again, his voice coming closer.

I turned my head slightly but before I could move further Teddy lifted the petrol can and thrust it in my direction.

"Don't you move a bloody step," he hissed. "I will fucking burn you before your friends can get here."

As if to emphasis his point, as if he needed to, he pulled a stainless steel lighter from his pocket, flipped open the top with his thumb and sparked up a flame. I felt all the warmth leave my body and my legs suddenly felt weak. I couldn't tear my eyes from the small flame that flickered like an aggressive creature in its own right. I could hear Peter walking across the living room and knew he would be here in mere moments. And then what? I fully expected Teddy to make good on his threat and try to burn me and I had no idea how I would stop him from doing so. I could try throwing myself backwards, but that would likely result in me knocking into Peter, the two of us falling to the ground and becoming easy targets for whatever the mad man before me decided to do next. The only other options that occurred to me seemed equally foolish and likely to end up getting myself chargrilled, but then beggars can't be choosers.

"Sorry, I didn't hear you," I yelled, my eyes fixed on Teddy. "There's no one in here, just more mess."

Teddy's nose wrinkled and his glare became even more acute, something I would not have thought possible, but he didn't immediately douse me and set me alight so I counted that as a win.

"Alright," Peter called back, "we should call this in and head back to the hospital. Looks like it was a wasted trip after all."

"Coming," I called, without actually moving a step.

I continued to stare at Teddy. I had managed to avert disaster for a few seconds but now I was right back in the same situation again. If I moved Teddy would more than likely carry out his threat, but if I stayed where I was someone would come to see what the holdup was and I was back to trying to throw myself out the half opened door before I ended up doing a Guy Fawkes impression. Again I went with the only other option I could see.

"Just go," I hissed through my teeth, while gesturing with my head in the direction of the door behind where Teddy stood.

The door, top half of which held a currently broken pane of glass that marked it as Teddy's point of entry, led out onto a tarmacked area that appeared to be a parking area for the estate. Clearly we had arrived before Teddy could finish his little one man crime wave, breaking and entering, vandalism, arson, and for some reason he had decided to stick around a bit longer rather than immediately exiting stage left. Maybe he had been hoping we would take one look at the living room and leave so that he could carry on with his plan and head off in his own time. Or perhaps he had been worried that opening the door would have made too much noise and have alerted us to his presence. Whatever the reason he had definitely overstayed his welcome and it was high time he got out of there, for everyone's sake.

Teddy turned his head ever so slightly and his eyes darted in the direction of the door for an instant before returning to me. I could practically see his brain working as he weighed up his options before coming to a conclusion. Moving at almost glacial speeds he took a small step backwards toward the door. Though I was still a very long way from being out of trouble I felt a wave of relief wash over me at the tiny movement. My Hail Mary plan was working.

And of course that was when the door swung open behind me and Peter walked in.

"What's going on in here?" he said, as he stepped up behind me.

His eyes took in the situation in an instant. He saw Teddy standing there, petrol can in hand, anger radiating from every pore, his fight or flight response currently still undecided but wavering from the former to the latter, and proceeded to bark out the two most inappropriate words he could possibly have said at that moment.

"Drop it."

The Cheshire cat grin appeared on Teddy Taylor's face in an instant.

"Whatever you say," he said.

And with that he threw the petrol can and the still burning lighter down at my feet.

20

"Fire in your heart and love in your soul can drive you to do great things."
The Wisdom of Zhu Zhuang, No. 381

Option A it was then.

I threw myself backwards with all the strength my shaking legs could muster and slammed into Peter sending him sprawling. At the same moment the petrol can hit the floor and mercifully stayed up right, though the impact did send a gout of petrol sloshing from the open cap, over the kitchen floor, onto the carpet and, much to my horror, across my feet. Then the lighter struck the ground.

In my mind there was a whooshing sound as the

petrol ignited, though in reality I could hear little over the blood rushing in my ears and the panicked, whining sound that someone was making very close to the exact place where I was lying. Fire spread out from the point of impact like a wave when you throw a rock into a pond. It engulfed most of the kitchen floor in an instant and rushed hungrily forward to devour the petrol-soaked carpet and my waiting feet.

I scrambled backwards, practically climbing over Peter who was struggling to get back up himself, and just managed to get my feet clear when the fire reached the carpet. I'd once dropped a burning log from my fire at home onto the carpet and while it had certainly left its mark the carpet itself had barely burned at all. It seems that the missing ingredient it needed to really get it going was petrol. The area covered with the flammable liquid erupted immediately sending up a billow of blueish black smoke. The carpet around this started to blacken with alarming speed as it too began to burn and add its own cocktail of hazardous chemicals to the mix.

There was a bang and I looked up in time to see the back-door slamming shut and Teddy beating a hasty retreat down the road.

"Get off me," cried Peter, rolling me sideways with a shove of his arms.

I pitched onto a pile of assorted debris as Peter scrambled to his feet. For a second I thought he was going to run head long into the flames but as soon as he had confirmed which direction Teddy was running in he turned and sprinted for the front door, pulling his mobile phone from his pocket as he did so, and all but shouldering Mark out of the way in the process.

"Deal with that," he yelled, pointing towards the fire as he raced out the door.

I looked back at the burning heap of stuff scattered across the kitchen floor. Ok, sure.

"Get up you idiot," Rachel screamed, grabbing at my coat and trying to drag me to my feet.

With her help I clambered back to my feet and was finally able to put a bit of distance between myself and the flames. As I stood there like an idiot trying to get my breath back Rachel started grabbing things from the floor and unceremoniously tossing them to the far side of the room.

"Move anything that might burn," she ordered. "Jesus, Steve snap out of it and help. Mark go get some water, a wet towel, something to fight the fire with."

Mark rushed back through the door to the rest of the house and I finally got myself together enough to help Rachel with moving things out of the path of the approaching fire. I was grabbing up a rug, the corner of which had already started to smoulder, when my brain started working well enough to realise something it really should have figured out a lot sooner.

"Oh shit."

I scrambled forward at the same moment that Mark came running back into the room carrying a waste bin full of water. He rushed for the kitchen, but I was already a step ahead of him. Very much aware that my shoes were still covered with petrol I leapt over the burning part of the carpet, landing heavily beside the open kitchen door and crashing into the wall with enough force to knock the wind out of me. As Mark brought his arms back to cast the water into the flames, I grabbed the kitchen door and slammed it shut. Most of the water splashed harmlessly against the door, though enough of it landed on the carpet to effectively dowse the flames there.

"What the fuck?" he yelled at me. "Why did you do –"

At that moment the petrol can exploded.

Thankfully the closed kitchen door took the brunt of it, but the blast was strong enough to send it flying open again and Mark, throwing up his hands to protect his face, was sent staggering back by a powerful wall of hot air that came roiling out through the open doorway. I scrambled away from the heat as well, moving back toward the centre of the living room. The kitchen was now an inferno and it seemed to me as if every surface was ablaze. Things had gone way beyond anything Mark's bin full of water could deal with.

"We have to get out of here," Mark coughed, as more and more smoke started to fill the room.

Rachel, her hand pressed over her mouth, looked up at the dark cloud now crawling across the ceiling.

"Why hasn't the fire alarm gone off?" she yelled over the growing sound of the fire.

I looked up and scanned the ceiling but could see no sign of a smoke detector. It didn't seem right to me that someone like Irene wouldn't have one and so, with a sinking feeling in my stomach, I turned my eyes groundward. I found it almost immediately, smashed, like everything else in the room, by the wrath of Teddy Taylor.

"He broke the alarms," I cried. "No one else will know what's going on; we have to get people out of the building."

A look of horror spread across the two faces before me and I was sure that they, like me, were picturing the devastating fire that had dominated the news only a few short years ago and the many lives it had claimed. The building we were in was of a very different design to that twenty-four storey tower block, but there were still a lot of people crammed together in the adjoining flats, and without the fire alarm to give them a warning there was a good chance some of them wouldn't know about the fire until it was too late. I took one more look at the burning kitchen, trying desperately to think of something we could try to put the fire out, but it was way beyond the three of us now.

"Come on," I yelled, pushing the others ahead of

me towards the door.

We emerged coughing and blinking into the late afternoon light and I was struck by the realisation that we had only actually been inside the flat for a handful of minutes even though it felt like hours. Rachel had her phone out and was already calling the fire brigade. I looked down the street in the direction that Teddy, and presumably Peter, had headed but could see no sign of either of them. I turned back to Mark.

"Start banging on doors," I said in a tone that made it both a suggestion and a question. "You go left, I'll go this way."

Mark nodded and, running in opposite directions, we both headed for the front doors of the flats either side of the one belonging to Irene Thompson and Douglas Fairchild. I reached the first door and hammered on it with the flat of my hand, yelling the word 'FIRE' over and over at the top of my voice. After twenty seconds or so of getting no response I moved on to the next flat in line. This time I only managed a single bang on the door when it swung open and a harassed looking Asian woman in a large woollen sweater and jogging bottoms glared out at me.

"Fire," I pretty much shouted in her face, "there's a fire, you have to get out of your house."

The woman gave me a sceptical look, as though I was trying to play some sort of trick on her, but then she sniffed the air and caught a whiff of smoke. She took a single step out of her front door, looked off to her right and caught sight of the black clouds now pouring out of the doorway of the flat just two doors down. The blood drained from her face and she turned immediately and, much to my shock, ran back into her flat. I was about to follow, to yell at her again that she needed to leave, when she came rushing back out carrying a tiny dog that immediately started yapping for all it was worth. Leaving the woman and her dog to it I ran on to the next house and started up with the hammering routine again.

The eclectic collection of loud music was still blaring from several windows, but despite this some people had clearly heard all the noise I was making as doors further down the row were opening and people were starting to emerge on their own. A few of them, once they realised what was happening, also took up the cry and started banging on their neighbour's doors before I could reach them. Seeing this I chose instead to sprint past the remaining ground floor flats to the set of stairs that ran up to the second level of the building. I took the stairs two at a time, part of my mind telling me my leg muscles were going to regret that choice later, and upon reaching the top I went right back to banging on the doors of this new row of flats.

I was about a quarter of the way along when I realised with alarm that smoke now appeared to be coming from one of the flats on this level as well, the one directly above the one belonging to Mark's mum. This turn for the worst did have one upside however as the working smoke detectors in this flat were activated and all at once a wailing shriek started up in every flat in the building and in no time doors were opening on all three levels and people were rushing to get clear.

As people pushed past me I kept staring at the door of the second burning flat, waiting to see if anyone came running out. After about thirty seconds without any movement from that direction I let out a soft curse and moved rapidly towards the smoking flat. I reached the door and once more started banging.

"Hello," I yelled, "hello, is anyone in there?"

There was no answer, and so I moved to the window and tried to get a look inside. There were no lights on in the flat and it took me a moment for my eyes to adjust enough to make anything out. Once they did I could see that the place was decorated in a far more modern style than the one below it, with the focus of the room being a large, flat screen television mounted on the right hand wall. Smoke rolling out from the kitchen and areas of the cream carpet close to it were starting to darken before my eyes. I cast my eyes around the room but could see no sign that anyone was inside, the place appeared empty.

At that moment there was the shrill cry of a siren from off to my left and I turned to see a fire engine racing down the street. The sight of it almost made me weep with joy and I turned to run back down the walkway to the stairs.

"*NO!*"

The voice, that was both female and most definitely not mine, sounded so loud inside my head that it almost staggered me to my knees. My ears seemed to ring with it even though it was clear that the sound was not coming from the world outside my brain. I let out a gasp. I'd never experienced anything like it before, and yet there was something familiar about the sensation, something that brought to mind long nights of sitting at my desk, pen in hand, waiting for ideas to come. I steadied myself on the wall and turned back to face the door to the burning flat. I knew I had missed something and before I could talk myself out of it I raised my foot and kicked out at the door with all my might.

21

"Friendships, like iron, are strongest once they have been forged in the flames."
The Wisdom of Zhu Zhuang, No. 1429

I learnt something in that moment. Kicking a door open is not as easy as they make it look in the movies. It's harder, it hurts, and it doesn't always work first time. To my credit the door did make a cracking sound close to the lock, however most of the forces involved rebounded onto me and I pretty much bounced back, flailing my arms wildly and only just managing not to fall on my arse. Thank you, Mr Newton. But I wasn't about to give up, I needed to get inside and so, giving my leg a quick rub, I steadied myself, actually bothered to take proper aim this time, and kicked out again.

I was rewarded with another loud crack and after another few kicks that left my leg throbbing the frame around the door was starting to break and a gap a couple of inches wide had opened up. Unfortunately, this also allowed more of the smoke building up inside the flat to escape right into my face. I quickly found myself in the unenviable position of engaging in a physically demanding task whilst having to hold my breath the best I could at the same time. After every kick I had to take a step back to draw in some air, which resulting in a great deal of unpleasant coughing and spluttering each time. Gathering myself once more I kicked out again and suddenly the door gave way, leaving me subject to Mr Newton's first law this time. I stumbled forward into the entrance hall, momentarily blinded by a gust of smoke, tripped over a pair of shoes that someone had clearly set as a trap for me, and for the second time that day found myself bashing painfully into a wall.

Righting myself while hissing out a string of inventive curses, I pushed through the half open door to the living room and walked into the flat proper. The room was rapidly filling with smoke, though at present it was still pooling in the upper half of the room and so I was able to avoid the worst of it by walking stooped over. Now that I was inside I had a better view of the place and it was clear to me I was within the dwelling of a male of the species. In addition to the massive telly there was a black leather sofa with a matching reclining armchair, an expensive looking stereo system, two different games consoles, and a shelving unit full of nothing but video games and Blu-rays. I found myself hoping the guy had insurance; he was going to need it.

Keeping low I moved toward the kitchen first, skirting around the dark patches on the carpet. Reaching it I carefully pulled the door open a bit further and looked inside. Layout wise it was identical to that of the flat directly below it, though again the pile of dirty dishes in the sink, the boxes of sugary cereal, and the multipacks of crisps on the worktop told me a lot about the person who lived here. But far more importantly the kitchen was currently not on fire, though smoke was rising up through the floor at an alarming rate. Thankfully there was no sign of anyone in the kitchen because I wasn't entirely sure I would have been able to get to them had there been.

Moving back across the living room I headed for the other door that I knew from listening to Mark downstairs more than likely led to at least one bedroom and a bathroom. The smoke was getting thicker and I was starting to find it harder to breath. My head felt like someone was slowly filling it with cotton wool and there were spots appearing at the edge of my vision. Leaning against the side of the sofa I pulled up the top of my jumper so that it was over my mouth and nose and took a breath. It didn't help that much, but I was able to get enough air into my lungs to make the spots go away and my head to clear up a bit. Knowing things would only get worse the longer I waited I pushed myself off the sofa and fumbled my way through the door.

The corridor beyond the door was narrow and had three doors leading off of it. Two close together towards the middle of the left-hand wall, and one at the end that, given the door was wide open, I could see led to the bathroom. Leaning against the right-hand wall to steady myself I made my way towards the first of the two doors. My arm knocked into something, there was a clatter, and something fell to the floor. I looked down to see a now broken photo frame lying there. Looking back up I saw the whole wall was lined with the things. I glanced at the image in the first one.

And froze.

A gasp escaped my throat and I felt my insides tighten in a way that had nothing to do with the dangerous amounts of smoke I was inhaling. My eyes locked onto the face of the person in the picture. I knew that face, knew it almost as well as my own. That smile, those eyes, the hair. It was all intimately familiar to me and I knew I would recognise it until my dying day. What I couldn't fathom however was what it was doing here, on the wall of an estate flat in Peckham? Why would a stranger have a picture of my Laci, my wife, the undisputed love of my life, hanging on their wall?

The answer came to me in an instant and suddenly I was moving once more. I slammed open the nearest door and stared around the room beyond. There was a computer desk, a weight bench and several cardboard boxes in the corner but that was it. I moved quickly to the next one and threw open the door. Or at least I tried to. The door hit something when it had opened about a foot and bounced back. I blocked it with my arm before it slammed in my face and this time leant my weight against it and pushed. I had a dreadful feeling building inside me that I knew what was blocking the door and if I was right there was no time to spare.

The spots were back in my vision and I was coughing almost constantly now, but I kept pushing and slowly, inch by inch, I managed to widen the gap until, finally, it was big enough to squeeze through. I forced my body through and as I slid clear I immediately fell to the ground. God my head felt heavy and all I wanted to do was have a short rest, just close my eyes for a bit while I gathered my strength. But I knew that was suicide and so, with a great deal of effort, I managed to force my increasingly weary body into a sitting position and turned to look at what was blocking the door.

The man was lying face down on the floor, dressed in jogging bottoms and a t-shirt. I crawled over to him, grabbed his shoulder, and pulling with all the strength I could muster, I managed to roll him over, knowing who I would find even before I saw his face.

"Darren," I yelled, "wake up mate, come on, I'm not sure I can carry you out of here."

There was no response. I reached down and pressed two fingers against his neck and tried to calm the beating of my heart enough for me to make out the beating of his. It was there, but it was weak. I leant down and pressed my ear close to his mouth and was relieved to find that he was still breathing as well, as I didn't think I would have been able to give him CPR in the state I was in.

"Darren," I shouted again, shaking his shoulders as I did so, "you've got to wake up; we've got to get out of here."

Darren let out a groan and his eyes cracked open a fraction. He stared at me through heavy lids for a moment and his forehead wrinkled in confusion.

"Steve?" he said, his voice slow and heavy. "What are you doing here?"

I smiled; I couldn't help it.

"Plenty of time for that later mate, right now we need to get out of here."

I bent and managed to get his arm over my shoulder and, straining, pulled him up into a sitting position. Working together, and using the end of the bed for help, we both managed to clamber to our feet, though it was immediately clear to me that there was no way Darren would be able to walk to the front door without help. Supporting as much of his weight as my aching legs and lungs could manage we slowly, step by step, headed out of the bedroom and down the corridor. We passed the picture of Laci, my wife, Darren's sister, and I swear she was smiling more than when I had looked earlier. We reached the living room, Darren supporting me now almost as much as I supported him, and we walked in to find that the fire had finally arrived.

"Fucking hell!" Darren cried, stumbling to a halt as he took in the raging flames rapidly consuming the far end of his living room.

"Come on," I shouted, dragging him towards the front door and safety.

We picked up the pace as best we could, trying not to focus all our attention on the fire growing ever closer. We were almost there when the floor seemed to buckle beneath us, tilting in the direction of the fire and suddenly Darren lost his balance and was falling, dragging me with him. I hit hard, knocking free what little air remained in my lungs as my chest hammered into the floor. I opened my mouth, trying to draw in a breath, but there didn't seem to be any air to be found and I started coughing violently, my body shaking with every convulsion of my lungs. My vision was going dark at the edges now and I could feel my head being drawn downwards as if it were doubling in weight with every passing second. I managed to twist it to the side and could see that Darren was in a similar condition, barely able to hold his head more than an inch above the floor.

I don't really know what happened next. I couldn't tell you if it was real or was a result of the lack of oxygen getting to my brain, but all at once Darren was no longer lying beside me and in his place was a woman, a woman with the same coloured eyes, the same high cheek bones.

"Get up," said Laci.

I stared at her just taking her in and she rolled her eyes in the way she always used to whenever I was doing something annoying.

"Hey, don't ignore me," she said, a sweet smile playing on her lips. "Up you get now, there's not much time left."

I felt moisture building at the corners of my eyes despite the growing heat.

"I'm so tired," I told her, "can't I just stay here for a little while with you?"

Laci's smile turned sad.

"I'd like that, but no, you need to move now."

"I miss you so much," I told her, as the tears started to run down my cheeks. "Everything is so hard without you, if I can just rest; just stay here then we can be together again."

Tears blossomed in her eyes as well.

"I know, I miss you too, but it's not your time yet."

Her face grew stern; her jaw setting in a way I'd seen many times before and which always made it clear that her mind was set.

"Now come on, no more messing about," she said, struggling to keep her voice from cracking. "I've gone through too much for you to give up on me with the job only half done. Get on your feet, do it now, do it for me. Please Steve, I love you so much, I don't want to see you die like this."

I tried to push myself up but it was simply too hard, my body felt like it was tied down with steel cables.

"I can't," I said, "it's too much, I miss you too much, I don't want to leave you."

At this Laci's tears started to flow, but her face grew angry.

"Steve Joseph Lander," she snapped, "if you let my baby brother die here, if you let yourself die here, I promise you that you will never, ever find me in the next life."

That hurt, more than any of the physical pains my body was feeling. It felt like my already broken heart had been shattered all over again. Until today I have never believed in an afterlife, as far as I was concerned when we die we are just gone, like a blown light bulb. When Laci died she simply stopped being, she didn't move on somewhere new, I just lost her forever. But now, and in the face of everything that had happened today, that piece of my philosophical outlook crumbled, demonstrable evidence accomplishing what years of argument with Laci never could. I now fully believed that an afterlife existed and that Laci was there waiting for me. And now she was threatening to take that away from me again.

Gritting my teeth I pushed with all my remaining strength, struggling to lift myself from the ground. My body screamed in protest and the concrete filling my head called to me to give in and lay back down again. But none of that compared to the power of my fear of losing Laci forever. Growling through my teeth I managed to raise myself onto all fours. I turned to look for Laci but she was gone again and in her place lay Darren once more. I reached out and grabbed the collar of his t-shirt.

"Crawl," I managed to croak out.

I started moving, dragging at Darren's collar, not even waiting to see if he had heard me. His weight felt colossal, especially when it was all I could do to support my own body, and I wasn't sure how much further I could go if I had to support both of us. But then the burden lessened and looking back I saw that Darren was looking my way and was making an effort to follow me towards the door. Keeping hold of his collar I turned back towards our goal and focused on nothing but moving one limb at a time, inching my way closer and closer to safety.

I am sure to an outside observer the whole thing would have seemed trivial. In reality I doubt we were more than a couple of feet at most from the entrance hall, and then only a few more from making it outside. Darren's flat simply wasn't big enough for the distances involved to be more than that. But for me it felt like every inch was a mile and that the journey was uphill all the way. But we kept at it and several hours later, or maybe two minutes depending on your perspective, we crossed over into the entrance hall. The smoke was still thick here, mainly by virtue of it being drawn out of the front door as if it were a chimney, but down towards the ground the air was relatively clear and for the first time in ages I was able to draw in a desperate deep breath.

"Not far now," I said to Darren.

He nodded back at me, clearly enjoying the same revitalising sensation of actually being able to breathe as I was. Compared to the journey from the living room those last few feet felt easy. It was still hard, but with every breath I took I felt strength flowing back into me and, all at once, we were outside on the balcony again and the smoke was rising up and away from us. I rolled over so that I was sitting on the ground and helped Darren the rest of the way. We both shuffled back until we were sitting with our backs to the balcony railing, watching the clouds of black billow out of Darren's front door. After a millennium or two Darren spoke.

"You saved my life."

I managed a smile and patted his shoulder in response.

"How did you know I lived here?"

I chuckled and shook my head.

"I didn't," I said, "had no idea at all."

Darren looked confused.

"Then why are you here?" he asked.

I broke into a broad smile at this.

"It's a long story, one with some very unusual props."

I patted the pocket holding the remaining cookies to illustrate my point. My blood froze. I looked down to confirm what my fingers had already told me. The bag containing the three remaining fortune cookies and, I had absolutely no doubt about it now, the last three messages from Laci, was gone. I stared up at the gaping black smoking maw that was Darren's front door in horror. And then I did something stupid, monumentally, epically, earth shatteringly stupid.

I pulled myself back to my feet and without another word to Darren I ran back into the fire.

22

"Years apart can do nothing to temper a close friendship."
The Wisdom of Zhu Zhuang, No. 261

This time round I at least had the sense to keep my head low and my arm pressed over my mouth and nose, give me some credit. I was through the entrance hall in an instant and back into the hell that the living room had become. The sofa was on fire now, as was a large part of the carpet. The heat was incredible and a foot into the room I was stopped in my tracks by it as suddenly as if I had run into yet another wall. I whispered up a prayer to the God I still very much didn't believe in, but was now at least willing to consider the possibility of, that the bag of cookies would be where I expected them to be and started scanning the living room floor around the area where Darren and I had fallen.

My prayer was answered, in part. The bag was there, right where I expected it to be. It was also very much on fire. The horror of the idea of losing this last connection to Laci pushed me on into the wall of heat and I dropped to the ground, batting at the burning mass with my hands in an attempt to put out the flames. The bag was done for, that much was clear and, though tragic, was a loss I was willing to live with. The cookies themselves were fairing slightly better, or at least two of them were. I snatched up the two intact, if far from pristine, cookies and shoved them into my pocket. The last one however was all but destroyed. The outer wrapping was blackened and charred, the ribbon having burn away completely causing the small package to split open and present its content to the flames. The cookie inside reminded me of one of my earliest attempts to bake the things and was burnt to a crisp. As for the fortune itself? I reached out, barely caring if I burnt my fingers, and searched desperately through the debris, but the fortune was gone. All that remained was a tiny piece of smoking vellum.

My heart sank, but there was no time to dwell on the loss now. The heat was intense and I needed to get out before the smoke overcame me again. I shoved the remains into my pocket with the two surviving cookies and pulled myself up and ran from the house. The journey took a matter of seconds this time and I marvelled at how much effort it had taken before, the whole experience already starting to feel like a dream. I burst from the flat into the open air and doubled over, hands on my knees, breathing hard.

"What the fuck man?" Darren screamed at me. "What the hell was all that about."

I didn't answer straight away; instead I reached into my pocket, pulled out one of the two remaining cookies, and held it out to him.

"Here," I gasped, "this belongs to you."

He took the cookie and looked at it dumbfounded. I looked up and saw the expression on his face and chuckled.

"Just keep it safe," I said, "I'll explain later."

Darren held out the cookie, dangling it between thumb and forefinger.

"You couldn't have grabbed the TV instead?"

I laughed at this as I slumped down beside him, I couldn't help myself, and pretty soon Darren joined me. We were both still sitting there, stupidly only a few feet from the burning flat, laughing our heads off when, a few moments later, a couple of fire fighters came rushing over, pulled us to our feet and ushered us along the balcony, down the stairs and to safety. Rachel and Mark came hurrying over as soon as we made it onto the pavement.

"God, Steve, are you alright?" Rachel asked with genuine concern in her voice as she looked me over.

I looked down at my smoke-stained clothes and over at Darren's dirty, barely recognisable face and could well understand her concern if I looked anywhere near as bad as he did. I opened my mouth to answer but instead started coughing violently, doubling over slightly at the pain in my lungs. Darren placed a steadying hand on my shoulder and the emotion that rushed through me at that small, simple gesture was almost overwhelming.

"Easy there man," Darren said, both concern and humour in his voice, "don't you go dying on me now, alright?"

Slowly I managed to get my coughing under control and straightened back up, to find Rachel staring intently at Darren, her mouth doing that fish thing that I was so good at.

"Darren?" she asked hesitantly. "Is that you?"

Darren looked at her, blinked a few times as if he were having trouble focusing, and broke into a broad smile.

"Rachel," he exclaimed, "wow, this is crazy, first Steve then you. What are you doing here? I haven't seen you in, well, what has it been, it seems like forever."

Rachel smile.

"Yeah, it's been a while, probably getting on for six years or so."

"Wow that long, really? Well it's great to see you;

you look as amazing as always."

Rachel laughed, brushing a stray hair behind her ear.

"Thanks, it's great to see you too, though I must say you've looked better."

Now it was Darren's turn to laugh. He looked down at his filthy clothes and body, made a show of brushing off the smallest amount of the dirt off of each shoulder, took a step forward and opened his arms wide. For a moment Rachel stood there smiling and shaking her head and then, as I once more reclaimed the fish impression as my own, she stepped into his embrace and wrapped her arms around him. After what seemed to me way too long for just a friendly hug I couldn't hold back my curiosity any more.

"So, I take it you two know each other?"

They both turned towards me, breaking apart with apparent reluctance. Was Rachel blushing?

"We…" said Darren, pointing at Rachel.

"Yes, we," said Rachel helpfully.

They looked at each other, laughed, and spoke in unison.

"Durham."

It took a moment for my smoke addled brain to catch up, but then I recalled that as a younger man Darren had attended university in Durham, and that Rachel had mentioned doing likewise earlier that morning.

"I see," I said.

Darren smiled, and yup, Rachel was definitely blushing.

"So," she said, once more fixing a stray hair, "how do you two know each other?"

I looked over at Darren, suddenly feeling embarrassed.

"Umm, he's my, well we, umm, well..." I stammered, suddenly unsure in what relational manner I was meant to refer to a man I had effectively pushed out of my life years ago.

Darren however didn't seem to have this issue.

"I'm his brother in law," he said.

I felt my heart swell at this and looked at him afresh. It seemed that, for him at least, the years apart and the loss of his sister hadn't stopped him considering me family. I suddenly found myself remembering all of those unreturned calls he had made to me over the years, calls I had always let go to voicemail and deleted without listening to them. He had never stopped reaching out to me; I had simply refused to respond.

"Your brother in law?" Rachel exclaimed. "Did you know he lived here?"

I shook my head.

"I had no idea."

Rachel smiled.

"Fortune cookies?"

"Fortune cookies," I agreed.

Darren looked at us both.

"I have no idea what you two are talking about

and I am not sure this one," he hooked a thumb in my direction, "is entirely sane, but right now I am ok with that. I take it you and Steve are friends?"

Rachel nodded.

"Yes, well no, well I think so. Technically I only met him this morning and a heck of a lot has happened since then, but yeah, I think he is someone worth having as a friend."

"I always thought so," said Darren, slapping me on the back this time and setting off another coughing fit.

I turned and looked back at the burning building, which had apparently slipped my mind amidst all the day-time soap opera drama, and watched as the fire brigade fought the flames, even now starting to bring them under control.

"Did we get everyone out?" I asked between coughs.

Rachel turned and exchanged a look with Mark before answering.

"We think so, once the alarm went off most people came running out on their own. As far as we can tell right now everyone got out before the fire could spread too far."

I closed my eyes for a moment and nodded my head slowly. That was good news at least.

"What about Peter?" I asked, before looking over at Mark. "What about Teddy."

Mark's face was a kaleidoscope of emotion. He looked heartbroken at the loss of his family home, ecstatic that we had managed to stop anyone from getting seriously hurt and enraged that the fire had been the result of his father's actions, all at the same time. There was also a sense of triumph, a small and slightly wicked smile that kept turning up the corners of his mouth. I knew the answer to my question before anyone said anything.

"They're over there," said Rachel, pointing off down the road.

I turned my head in the direction she indicated to see Peter standing beside a patrol car and next to a uniformed police officer who was busy bundling an angry handcuffed Teddy Taylor into the back of the vehicle.

"They'll put him back inside for this," growled Mark, though there were tears at the corner of his eyes even as he vented his anger.

"Is that who started the fire?" Darren asked me, resting a hand back on my shoulder as the coughing started up again.

I nodded by way of an answer as I concentrated on my breathing.

"I'm glad they got the bastard," Darren said.

Mark let out a grunt.

"Me too," He added, as he rubbed what I fully expected were the last tears he would shed for his father from his eyes with the back of his hand.

At that moment a couple of paramedics came hurrying over and started fussing around me and Darren who, judging from the people I could see milling around, had suffered the most in the fire. We were led, politely but forcefully, in the direction of an ambulance that sat idling on the kerb a few vehicles down form the fire engine, and had oxygen masks pressed over our mouths which, I have to admit, did make breathing a hell of a lot easier. I pulled my mask off for a moment and yelled over to Rachel as the paramedics helped me up into the back of the ambulance.

"Get Peter and meet us at the hospital. I don't think this is finished yet."

23

"True family doesn't care what you did wrong; it is always there, waiting to forgive."
The Wisdom of Zhu Zhuang, No. 981

With masks over our faces Darren and I didn't talk much on the ride to King's College Hospital. As such I took the time to run over the events of the day in the light of what, up until now, had been the missing piece of the puzzle, the source of the messages. I was sure that Peter's idea about me having engaged in some form of automatic writing when creating my fortunes was correct. And now, after what I had experienced in Darren's flat, I knew that the voice that had been whispering in my ear as

I put calligraphy pen to vellum had belonged to Laci, my dearly departed.

Why she had chosen to communicate with me in such a convoluted way was beyond me. Laci had always been forthright and direct in life, so why the shell, or more accurately cookie, games now? The best I could come up with was the idea that wherever she was there were rules governing her interaction with the mortal realm. I had long considered the stylings of self-proclaimed psychic mediums to be good evidence against the existence of an afterlife. Why, if they really were in touch with the other side, would Great Aunt Agnes, who never forgot a thing during her days on earth, suddenly have such difficulty in communicating her own name, only being able to offer up the fact that it might begin with an A, or maybe an S. To me this had always indicated evidence of fraud, but now I was questioning that assumption. I felt sure now that some sort of spiritual existence was real, an existence in which the dead had access to knowledge far beyond that of the living. As such perhaps there was a moratorium upon direct, clear communication. Maybe the best the dead could do was offer hints, suggestions, and generalities and hope that whoever was listening was smart enough to work out what they were trying to say. Of course I had absolutely no way of proving that any of this was the case, and I could already see several holes in my own explanation, but somehow the general shape of it felt right to me, so I decided to run with it.

It seemed to me that, with these hypothetical restrictions in place, Laci had reached out to me from the great beyond. Looking back, I felt sure I could pinpoint the first time she tried, or at least the first time I heard her. It was that day I had awoken suddenly from a troubled sleep just in time to catch a baking show on TV about fortune cookies. That moment had arguably saved my life, as without that new fascination to throw myself into I would have more than likely slipped every deeper into depression and despair. In that moment there had been a spark, a flickering ember of the blazing fire of love and joy I had experienced with Laci, and for the first time since her passing I had felt like I might, just might, be able to go on without her.

And then, once I allowed myself to relax enough, to be open enough, Laci started speaking to me in earnest. Still unable to communicate with me in her usual direct and forthright fashion she had instead inspired me to write message to others, vague, meaningless, easily missed messages that the powers-that-be that governed her new reality allowed her to pass on. And so, through me, Laci threw breadcrumbs out into the world, hoping someone would eventually pick up on them and seek me out. And they had. Detective Inspector Peter Fuller of the Metropolitan Police Service had seen those breadcrumbs and over two years had gathered them together until they formed a pile that couldn't be ignored anymore. After that, as Laci had intended, he had come to find me so that her real message could be, equally cryptically, relayed.

And so, Laci led Peter to me, and we in turn were led to Rachel. Rachel then led us to first Douglas Fairchild, and then Terry Taylor, and then the rest of the Taylor family. And the Taylor family led me to Darren, Laci's brother, at his moment of greatest need, a moment where, had I not been there, he would have likely died in the fire set by Teddy Taylor. But there he was, sitting across from me looking worn and sullen but very much alive. Yes, I had played my part, but it was Laci who had directed me, guiding me step by step while at the same time adhering strictly to the rules of whatever and wherever it was that governed how she was and was not allowed to communicate with me. She had saved the life of her little brother and had brought me back into contact with the family I had abandoned in the selfishness of my grief. A family who, it seemed in Darren at least, still held its arms open to me, waiting for me to come back into the fold.

But she had done more than that, she had also brought me back into contact with someone else from my past, someone else I had avoided in the years since her death and who, on this strange and miraculous day, was once more in my life. Dr Mackenzie Hanson.

We arrived at the hospital and were unloaded from the back of the ambulance and directly into a couple of wheelchairs. We both insisted we felt well enough to walk, and in turn were informed that doing so was not an option, and so were wheeled into the hospital and to a couple of examination beds where we were at least allowed to get up and climb onto the beds without assistance. A nurse told us that a doctor would be along to see us in due course, and we were left to it.

"Well," said Darren, "I guess we probably aren't dying."

"Doesn't look like it," I agreed. "But NHS cutbacks being what they are who can tell."

We both smiled. God it was good to see him again. Though he was a good few years younger than me and Laci I had always gotten on well with Darren and I hadn't realised how much I had missed him being a part of my life until just now. I guess his sister had used up all the resources I'd had available for missing people, and once I cut myself off from her family it became easier not to think about them at all. After a few more moments of merriment Darren's face suddenly grew serious.

"What happened to you man?" he asked. "You vanished from our lives; it was like we lost you too."

I felt a torrent of shame and sadness erupt inside me at his words. I had never even considered things from his point of view before, but now I could see how much extra pain my actions had inflicted on those people that cared about me the most. When I met Laci I found more than just the love of my life, I also found the family I had always dreamed of as a child. Laci's mum Mary had more genuine warmth and affection in her little finger than either of my actual parents combined, and her dad Tony had been more of a father to me than my own had ever been. And on top of that I had gained an amazing little brother in Darren. For some crazy reason he had always looked up to me. He would seek my advice on all manner of issues, as if I actually had a clue about anything, and would confide in me in a way that I am not sure he could do even with the actual members of his family. And in turn he was always there for me when I needed him, they all were. And in my moment of greatest need I had turned my back on them and walked away. In a way Laci's death hadn't just robbed them of a beloved daughter and sister; it had taken a son and brother from them as well. As the realisation of what I had done washed over me I felt my chest tighten and tears start to roll down my cheeks.

"I'm sorry," I choked, "I am so sorry, I never meant to hurt you, I just, I just lost my way without her."

"But you didn't have to go through it on your own," said Darren, tears appearing at the corner of his eyes as well. "We were there for you, we needed you. We were family man; family doesn't turn its back on one another like that."

My thoughts flashed to my father and his disappearance down under as if to offer a counter to this argument, but even as the idea formed in my mind I knew it was flawed. My father had been responsible for giving me life, that much was true, but he had never really been family, not in any way that mattered. Darren was right; after my mum died my real family had been him, and his parents, and Laci, and when I, when we, lost her I had walked away from them just like my biological father had walked away from my mother and me. I hated myself for that. I sniffed, trying to bring my emotions back under control.

"You're right, I was wrong, I was stupid and selfish and hurting and I should never have turned my back on you guys. But that's over, I don't expect you to forgive me or anything, but I honestly believe that Laci led me back to you and from now on, if you ever need me for anything I will be there, I'm not going to disappear again."

Darren turned his face away from me and rubbed at his eyes with the back of his hand. When he turned back his eyes looked red from more than just the smoke, but he was smiling.

"You're a bloody idiot you know that right?"

"Yeah," I agreed, as a smile forced its way onto my own lips.

Darren looked around him for a moment checking there was no one in sight.

"Ok quick, before anyone comes and gets the

wrong idea, give me a hug, stop being a prat and let's be done with all this stupid emotion stuff."

I laughed and almost started crying again at the same time. I swung my legs off the bed as Darren did the same and we both leant forward and gave each other an awkward and overly manly hug, too much pressure and lots of back slapping, before breaking apart and climbing back onto our respective beds, both now wiping at our eyes and studiously avoiding each other's gaze. In an obvious attempt to change the conversation Darren reached into his pocket and pulled out the fortune cookie I had given him earlier. He held it up towards me, dangling it by the ribbon and swinging it gently back and forth.

"So, you want to tell me what this thing is all about?"

I stared at the fortune cookie for a moment. There was so much to tell, so much that I knew would sound crazy, that I didn't know where to start, and as such I decided to skip straight to the punchline.

"Would you believe me if I told you that it contains a message from your sister? And that similar messages brought me to London today, for the first time in years, and led me to a flat that I didn't know existed until a few hours ago, just in time to rescue someone I care about but haven't seen in ages and didn't even know was living there from a fire? I know it sounds crazy but, well, there you go."

Darren studied me for a long hard minute, and then his eyes flicked to the fortune cookie still dangling from his fingers.

"This contains a message from Laci?" he said in hushed tones.

I nodded.

"Yes. And specifically a message to you, about something important to the course of the rest of your life."

Darren lowered the fortune cookie and placed it on his lap.

"Should I open it now?"

I shrugged.

"It's up to you. From my experience with these things you will know when you are meant to open it. If it feels right open it, if not, well then wait until it does."

Darren looked at the fortune cookie for a few moments and before starting to pull on the bow that bound the top of the wrapper together. Then he stopped.

"No," he said, "not yet, soon I think, but not yet."

He held the cookie up before his eyes again, looked at it for a moment longer with a puzzled expression on his face, and stuffed it back into his pocket. He blew out a breath as if suddenly exhausted.

"Wow, that was weird man, it was like I could hear Laci telling me to wait a bit, even though I really wanted to see what was inside. Do you know what I mean?"

I smiled and nodded.

"Yeah," I said my voice cracking slightly once more, "I've heard her speaking to me too."

Before I could tell him about my experience back at his flat a doctor and nurse team, the former female, the latter male, turned up to check us over. They seemed inordinately concerned about the fact that Darren had actually passed out but after a great deal of fussing about, getting us to breathe into things and listening to our chests with a stethoscope the doctor announced that we were fit to leave, though we were both under strict instructions to seek out medical attention immediately should we experience any problems breathing over the next 48 hours. We both clambered off of our beds and were once again forced to endure an unnecessary wheelchair ride. We made it almost all the way to the front entrance when a group of familiar faces intercepted us coming the other way.

"Jesus, you look half-baked mate," said Peter, with a wide smile.

"I feel it," I said smiling back, "another few minutes and you could have stuck an apple in my mouth and served me for Sunday lunch."

My poor joke prompted a round of laugher that had more to do with released tension than any real humour and then we all lapsed into the awkward silence of people who don't really know what to say to one another. It was Mark who got things moving again.

"I'm really glad to see you are all right, but if you'll all excuse me I need to get back to my family. I need to tell mum about her house, and, well about Teddy as well I guess. So, yeah, take care and see you later I guess."

He glanced at us all as if waiting to see if any of us had a reason for him to stay.

"Go on," said Peter, resting a big hand on Mark's shoulder, "go be with your family, we'll find you if we need anything."

Mark nodded, gave us all a strained smile and squeezed past my wheelchair and hurried off back down the corridor. We all watched him go for a moment, Darren and me twisting round in our wheelchairs, before the awkward silence descended upon us once again. This time it was Peter's turn to break it.

"Here," he said, handing over my bag that I'd left in the back of his car, "this is yours."

I took the bag, thanked him and hooked it over my shoulder.

"So now what?" Peter continued. "Rachel said you thought that something else was going to happen, that the fire wasn't the end of it."

I nodded.

"I know where the messages come from now, and I think that means there is one more thing left to do. I hope I am wrong, I really do, I'm not really sure how I'll handle it if I'm right, but this isn't over yet."

Peter looked at me for a moment and then nodded.

"Ok, I'm with you."

"Me too," said Rachel, "I mean it's not like there is any point in me going back to work now anyway. I called Rob on the way here to get him to reschedule my readings. Though admittedly it's not the best look when a psychic has to change their plans unexpectedly."

We all smiled.

"Well I guess I'm in too," said Darren. "I mean I have absolutely no idea what's going on right now or what this is all about, but if you need me I'm there."

I gave him a nod.

"Thanks," I said softly.

He shrugged.

"It's what family is for," he answered with a sardonic grin.

"Right," said the orderly pushing my wheelchair, "now that you have all got that sorted we really should stop blocking the corridor like this and get you good people on your way."

We all offered up sheepish apologies and the orderlies started wheeling Darren and me towards the entrance once more, Peter and Rachel falling in behind.

We almost made it to the door when the screaming started.

24

"Though it may take a lifetime, you will find the justice you seek."
The Wisdom of Zhu Zhuang, No. 451

The shrill sound of the scream was almost instantly joined by other voices, voices raised in anger and alarm. This time I didn't need a cryptic fortune or a voice from the other side to kick me into action. I leapt up from the wheelchair, ignoring the protestations of the orderly, and set off at once in the direction of the loud voices, my pace quickening with every step until I was running flat out down the hospital corridors.

Even without the voices to guide me I would

have known where I was going. In moments I found myself sprinting up the corridor that led to Douglas Fairchild's room, my smoke damaged lungs screaming at me to slow down. Up ahead I could see the source of the commotion. Standing like a Roman phalanx before the door to Douglas Fairchild's room was the Taylor family. Anna stood at the end of the little line closest to me, her hands clamped tight onto her son's shoulders, apparently holding him back from doing something stupid. Next to them was Mark, his face angry, his right hand up and thrusting a finger repeatedly forward as if to emphasise the words he was yelling. Lastly there stood Irene, implacable as ever, her face set in a withering gaze the power of which I could feel even without it being aimed in my direction. And on the other side of the corridor, separated from them by a growing number of hospital orderlies and nurses, stood the target of the Taylors' ferocity. Dr Hanson.

"Are you calling my mother a liar?" cried Mark.

Hanson, who had his hands held up in a placating manner, shook his head.

"Not at all Mr Taylor," he said in an inordinately calm voice. "I am simply saying that she is mistaken. Now if you would all calm down I am sure I can explain."

"I am not mistaken," Irene cut in, "I know what I saw, and I know what you were doing."

"I assure you Mrs Taylor; I was only trying to help Mr Fairchild, nothing more."

"Nonsense," snapped Irene, "I was a nurse for twenty-five years, and what you were doing was not helping."

I skidded to a halt and moved to stand next to Anna and Terry, instinctively knowing which side of the unexpected confrontation I should align myself with. Dr Hanson saw me and I saw relief wash across his face.

"Ah, Mr Lander, thank goodness. You know me, can you please explain to your friends here that I would never try to harm Mr Fairchild."

I stared at him for a moment without speaking and when I did my words were directed towards the Taylors.

"What's going on?"

"A simple misunderstanding," Hanson said before anyone else could respond, "I was just checking in on Mr Fairchild, he is my patient after all, and I seem to have upset Mrs Taylor."

"You were trying to hurt him," Irene cut in. "I'll not let you get away with this."

"And I assure you I was doing no such thing. Why would I?"

This question seemed to bring the Taylors up short for a moment. It was a good question. Hanson was a doctor, had been for a good few years as far as I knew, with an obligation to help his patients. He didn't seem to know Fairchild, or the Taylors for that matter, so what possible motivation could he have for wanting to hurt the man? Irene apparently had some medical experience and believed that Hanson's actions, whatever they had been, had not been those of a healer, and yet medicine was a constantly evolving field and as such it was entirely possible that she was simply unaware of whatever he had been doing and had simply jumped to the wrong conclusion. What little I knew of the woman told me that this was a stretch, and yet the issue of motive, or in this case an apparently lack of one, seemed to push things very much in Hanson's favour.

I looked at Hanson and saw the earnest and forthright expression on his face. He was clearly disturbed by Irene's accusation, and yet he faced it with the confidence and conviction that only comes from the knowledge that you are in the right. Or, and I felt my stomach churn as the thought occurred to me, the knowledge that you can talk your way out of it. I felt my thoughts picking up speed, as if tumbling down the rabbit hole that had just opened up in my mind. And why would someone believe that they could talk their way out of a situation like this? The only answer that I could come up with as I stared at Hanson, my hands starting to shake slightly and my insides twisting up into a knot, was that he had talked his way out of it before. I can't explain how I knew, and given the day I was having I wasn't going to rule anything out, but in that moment I knew he was lying, that Irene was right, and for some reason Hanson had indeed tried to hurt Fairchild, and what was more it was not the first time he had done something like that.

I staggered back a little and leant against the wall. Everything seemed to become muffled and I could no longer clearly hear the words that Hanson and the Taylors were saying. I was only half aware that other people were arriving, more members of the hospital staff who started trying to calm the Taylor family down, as well as Peter, Rachel and Darren who were walking quickly up the corridor towards the confrontation. It all seemed to be happening somewhere else around someone else, as if I were watching from the outside through a murky window, there but apart from the action. I turned my head and looked at the Taylor family. Irene still looked resolute but I could see that a trickle of doubt was starting to enter Mark's mind. Anna looked equal parts confused and upset, and the fight seemed to be physically draining out of Terry, his body almost deflating as he started to question whether his anger was justified. In short I could see Hanson, backed up by the other hospital staff, talking them round. I could see Hanson winning.

I don't remember putting my hand in my pocket and actively seeking out the burnt and tattered remains of the fortune that had all but been destroyed in the fire, but all at once it was in my hand and I found myself looking at it. There was little left of it, just a tiny piece of burnt vellum, only two little bits of information left, a name and a number. Darren was standing next to me now and was saying something but I couldn't hear him. Instead I swung my bag off my shoulder and balancing it awkwardly against the wall I opened it and pulled out the book I had taken from my office a million years ago that morning and started flipping through the pages.

The book was nothing special, simply a somewhat good quality pad of A4 lined paper that I'd had for a couple of years. I had only written on the right hand side of each page and with various different colours and levels of neatness, but there in my hands was a complete record of every fortune that I had come up with and that had found its way into one of my cookies. I flicked through the pages quickly and within seconds I found the one that corresponded to the number on the burnt bit of vellum.

"There is power in names," I read, "power to heal, to comfort, and to set right that which is wrong."

I felt my heart drop.

"What does that mean?" Darren said.

I turned and looked at him, realising that I had automatically read the words of the fortune out loud.

"I don't know," I said, feeling the sudden weight of failure settling upon me, "names are important I guess."

Darren looked down and the page and then back at me.

"What names?"

I started to answer to say that I didn't know but I stopped myself. An idea entered my mind. I slipped the book back into the bag, swung it back over my shoulder, and turned to face Hanson. Things seemed to have calmed down, and while there was still a great deal of tension in the air Hanson seemed to have relaxed. He was saying something, using medical words I didn't understand, but they were clearly working. I could see that even Irene was starting to doubt herself now. Mark was looking back and forth between her and Hanson as if trying to weigh up the evidence to work out who was telling the truth and from the pained expression on his face I could tell he was leaning towards the doctor.

I took a deep breath and closed my eyes. It took me a moment but I managed to push away thoughts of what was going on around me, blocking out my awareness of the voices, the smell of hospital detergent, the closeness of the bodies around me, until I felt the concerns of the day slowly drift away and my mind open. As I had many times when using this technique to write my fortunes I felt a sense of comfort settle around me, a warm, safe, familiar feeling that I now knew came from the connection to Laci that it enabled. And then I listened.

At first nothing happened. No words appeared in my head, no guidance from the other side was forthcoming. I took another deep breath and reached out to Laci, calling out to her in my mind, asking her to fill my head with the words, with the names, I needed.

"John Barnard," I said, my eyes still closed.

Another name entered my mind.

"Linda Mason."

I opened my eyes now. Everything seemed the same, everyone was still animated and talking at once, though now it seemed that the Taylors were more engaged with one another than they were with Dr Hanson. I turned and looked over at the doctor and found that Hanson himself was no longer saying anything, instead he was staring at me, his eyes wide, his mouth open and soundless.

"George Whetherton," I said, looking straight at him.

He gulped; I literally saw his Adam's apple jump up and down. He took a small step away from me.

"Saraka Patel."

Another step.

"Pamela Lewis."

"David Penny."

Sweat broke out on Hanson's forehead. I couldn't recall ever seeing the man sweat before, even during those long hot days in the hospital with Laci. He took another step back, angling slightly to put one of the orderlies between him and me.

"Aldane Brown."

Hanson's mouth opened as if he were going to say something but he forced it closed again.

"Joshua Morris."

Another step back, more hurried and obvious this time.

"Megan William-Reid."

Hanson's lips moved, I couldn't make out what he said, but there was fear in his eyes now.

"Yiannis Pavlou."

Hanson's lips moved again and this time I heard the word.

"Stop."

I didn't.

"Thomas Finlay."

"Marie-Anne Watson."

"Stop," he said again, louder this time.

He had now backed off a few more steps, and though everything outside of him, me and the voices was little more than a blur I could tell that the general hubbub had ceased and all eyes were focused on our confrontation.

"Tessa Clarke."

"Meera Shah."

"Stop."

"George McAllister."

"Stop it."

"Samual Browne."

"STOP IT."

"David Schwartz."

"I SAID STOP IT."

"Julie Micheletti."

"STOP IT, GOD DAMN YOU, STOP IT."

I stopped, one more name poised on my lips, one more name that I wasn't sure I had the strength to say. All eyes were on Hanson now, even those of the nurses and orderlies. The man was visibly shaking, sweat running down his face, his eyes wide, a hunted animal cornered by a predator. I moved towards him and the hospital staff parted before me, the doubts and confusion on their faces relaying their internal need to see this played out. I stopped a few feet away from him and our eyes locked. I looked into him and I knew, I just knew, that it was over, would be over, if I could just say two more little words. I opened my mouth and felt my throat close around the sounds. I swallowed hard, then again, and around a knot of emotion that I was sure would choke me the moment I spoke, I forced out one more name.

"Laci Lander."

Hanson crumbled. His legs gave way beneath him and he collapsed heavily to the floor. Tears flowed down his cheeks and he stared up at me in abject horror and defeat.

"How do you know their names?" he asked in a whisper.

"You killed them," I said, my own body starting to shake now as I felt the familiar fury build inside me.

"How do you know their names?" Hanson said again, and there was a gasp from one of the nurses at the noticeable absence of any attempt at denial.

"Why?" I croaked as I felt wetness form on my own cheeks.

Hanson shook his head, back and forth, back and forth, as if trying to dislodge my words from his mind.

"I was trying to help them, don't you understand that?" he whined.

I stared at him, letting the intensity of my gaze do more than any words could have.

"I never meant to hurt them, I meant to save them, you have to believe me. I'm a healer, I help people, it's what I do."

The words flowed from Hanson as though he were talking to a priest in a confessional; he seemed desperate to make me understand his actions, to have me absolve him of any wrong doing. He failed in both tasks. I couldn't understand what he had done, and I would never forgive him for hurting Laci.

"Why?" I asked again.

This time Peter answered.

"To be the hero," he said. "He hurt them so he could be the one to save them."

Hanson's eyes snapped to Peter and a look passed over his face as he realised everyone was looking at him, everyone could hear what he was saying. He swallowed and I saw him try to bring himself back under control.

"No," he stammered, "you don't understand."

Before he could say any more Irene stepped up beside me.

"Check the pocket of his scrubs," she said her voice solid as a rock. "The right hand one."

Hanson looked up at Irene and panic showed for a second on his handsome features. He tried to scramble backwards but Peter was too quick. He took a step forward, reached down and seized Hanson by the collar. Ever the professional he patted Hanson's pocket before, a plastic glove almost miraculously appearing in his hands, he reached carefully into the pocket and pulled out a syringe.

"I saw him trying to inject that into my Douglas's IV," Irene said, her chin lifted high in vindication.

Peter held up the syringe and gave it a little shake.

"There's nothing in it," he said, "only air."

There were murmurs from the medical staff and even I knew enough about medicine from TV to know the implications of such an act.

"You were trying to give him a heart attack," I said.

Hanson's eyes snapped to mine once more.

"I wanted to save him," he said, and I could tell by the sincerity in his gaze that he meant it.

That was enough for Peter. He wrapped the syringe up in the disposable glove and slipped it into his own pocket. He pulled Hanson to his feet and swung him round, producing a pair of handcuffs from inside his jacket.

"Dr Hanson, I am arresting you on suspicion of the attempted murder of Douglas Fairchild. You do not have to say anything, but it may harm your defence if you do not mention when questioned something which you later rely on in court. Anything you do say may be given in evidence. Do you understand?"

Hanson didn't reply, he just stared at the horror filled faces of his hospital colleagues, looking for someone to fight his corner. But he was alone; they had all heard what he had said.

"Dr Hanson," Peter said his voice forceful, "do you understand what I have said to you?"

This time Hanson responded. He nodded his head slightly.

"Yes, I understand."

I felt something shift inside me at that moment and I don't really remember what happened next. I staggered but Darren and Rachel were suddenly at my side, taking hold of me, keeping me upright. Hanson was taken away. The Taylors drew together, hugging and talking in soft voices. More and more hospital staff seemed to appear, many of whom wore suits rather than hospital scrubs, quickly followed by additional police officers. The three of us were separated and taken into different rooms to give statements. I don't know what I said, it was just a blur, but before I knew it I was outside the hospital, standing with Darren, Rachel, and the Taylor family, though Irene remained inside with Douglas. I looked up to see Peter walking across the carpark towards us.

"You ok?" he said, addressing the comment clearly to me. I must have looked in bad shape.

I nodded.

"What's going on with Hanson?" I asked.

Peter made a gruff sound in his throat.

"He lawyered up of course. Now that he's calmed down he is trying to spin a different story."

He paused for a moment as if unsure what to say next.

"I ran a quick check on some of those names you mentioned, the ones I could remember anyway. Obviously I will need to do a more thorough search to make sure I am looking at the right people, but even so I found three people who died suddenly in hospital in the last couple of years, cause of death on all three recorded as a heart attack as the result of an air embolism. I have no doubt we will find that Hanson's name is associated with all of them."

His eyes met mine for a moment and I could see genuine concern and sorrow in his gaze.

"I checked out Laci's record as well," he said softly.

I nodded.

"Cause of death, heart attack resulting from an air embolism," I said in response to his unasked question.

Our small group lapsed into silence at this. I jumped a little when Mark placed a heavy hand on my shoulder. I turned to face him and was surprised to see he appeared close to tears.

"Thank you," he said to me, though I couldn't understand why.

"Thank you," echoed Anna.

I tried to swallow but there was that damn lump in my throat again. Darren stepped up next, slapping a hand on my back and giving me a side on hug.

"Yeah mate," he said with a forced smile holding back his tears, "thank you. You got the bastard who took her from us."

I looked around at the small group of people, most of whom I had known for no more than a day, but all of whom I already considered firm friends. We were bound together, the seven of us, nine if you included Irene and Douglas, bound by sorrow, pain, and hand crafted fortune cookies made by an obsessive, grieving man who was apparently a little bit psychic. I lifted my head and looked up at the sky. I could feel Laci there with me again, though I somehow knew that this would be the last time. I closed my eyes and listened for the words. I knew what they would be before I heard them, and they both broke my heart and built it anew at the same time, and no I am not going to tell you what they were.

I opened my eyes and Laci left me. And then the tears came.

25

"Know you are loved."
The Wisdom of Zhu Zhuang, No. 1

The ten of us sat around the fireplace in my living room, talking, laughing, drinking wine and eating rich food. My dog Bob sat on the floor beside Terry where he received almost constant attention from the boy, as well as more than a few pigs in blankets from Terry's plate. Tortoise was being more aloof of course, having perched herself on top of the small bookcase in the far corner of the room, but she was sociable enough to accept a stroke or morsel of food from those who passed her by. Irene and Douglas, who was looking a million times better than when we had first met, sat together on the sofa next to Peter and his wife, Helen. The detective was smiling broadly and had probably consumed a little too much alcohol, but as the two of them were staying the night in my spare room I wasn't worried about him driving into a ditch on his way back to London.

Darren had claimed the armchair, and Rachel had claimed Darren's lap. The two of them were snuggled up close, carrying on their own conversation for the most part, and giggling at the private jokes of a couple in love. I glanced over at them from time to time, knowing in my heart that this was something else Laci had intended when she had whispered words into my mind as I attempted to use baking and craft to fill the void she had left in my life.

Mark, Anna and I were all seated in front of my small but generously decorated Christmas tree in chairs I had taken from the dining room. Anna was trying to convince a very reluctant Mark that they should get an open fire installed in their house and I for my part was thoroughly enjoying winding him up by offering my services as an architect to design the thing for them.

It had been the best part of eight months since the day my fortune cookies had brought us all together. The day when Douglas and Darren had almost died, and Dr Mackenzie Hanson, the man who killed my wife, had first been brought to account. The wheels of justice, slow turning as ever, had yet to bring about a formal conviction, though Peter assured me on a regular basis that it was a forgone conclusion and just a matter of time. Since his initial arrest the evidence against Hanson had built up steadily. Though he had not been charged in connection with the deaths of all nineteen of the names I had mentioned the police had uncovered enough evidence to bring formal charges against him in five of the cases, my beloved Laci amongst them. There was also a growing body of evidence to indicate that he had successfully induced a heart attack and revived at least a dozen more people over the years, though the police suspected this was only the tip of the iceberg.

While the Crown Court was yet to render its verdict the court of public opinion had been more than happy to do so. Hanson had been crucified by the press, who had of course labelled him the next Harold Shipman despite the differences in their crimes, and regardless of whatever else happened he would never work in a hospital in the UK again.

As for me, I had a family again and had started to pull myself back together. Through Darren I had reconnected with Laci's parents and had finally gotten it through my thick skull that I didn't have to deal with Laci's death alone. I wasn't ready to do anything as crazy as start dating again, and I was unsure if I would ever actually get to that stage, but I no longer felt alone, and with friends and family around me I knew I could keep going and that life would slowly, bit by bit, start to pull the shattered pieces of my heart back together. The cracks would always show, but I knew I would be whole again one day.

I hadn't written any more fortune cookies. A few months ago I had sat down to try but it had almost immediately become clear that whatever psychic connection I'd had to Laci was gone. I'd cried for a long time, but once I was done I had gathered up all of my calligraphy and crafting supplies and taken them down to a local charity shop. I didn't need them anymore, that part of my life was over, and while it was painful to do I had no doubt it had been the right thing.

Sitting there, surrounded by the bustle and noise of my friends, I glanced up at the fireplace where a framed picture of Laci sat in pride of place. I felt a familiar tug of pain at my heart, but it was tempered now by the love I still felt for her and the countless good memories of our time together. I could no longer hear her speaking to me, but the sound of her voice was something I would never forget. Besides, I knew for sure now that I would see her again one day, of that I was certain. Plus, there on the mantel piece beside her picture, partially burnt and somewhat worst for wear, sat an unopened fortune cookie. I had no idea when I would be led to open it, or even if it was my place to do so. But I knew that it contained Laci's words and that, when the time came, I would follow them wherever they may lead.

Printed in Great Britain
by Amazon